THE INFAMOUS Frankie Lorde

NO ADMISSIONS

CHECK OUT ALL OF FRANKIE'S "MARKS"

Book 1: **STEALING GREENWICH**

Book 2: **GOING WILD**

BRITTANY GERAGOTELIS

PIXEL+INK

PIXEL+INK

Pixel+Ink is an imprint of TGM Development Corp.

www.pixelandinkbooks.com

Printed and bound in July 2022 at Lake Book Manufacturing

in Melrose Park, IL, U.S.A.

Book design by Steve Scott and Jay Colvin

Cataloging-in-Publication information is available from the Library of Congress.

Hardcover ISBN: 978-1-64595-123-0

E-book ISBN: 978-1-64595-124-7

First Edition

1 3 5 7 9 10 8 6 4 2

For Matty

Entry One

Of all our plans, this was by far the craziest.

And it's my own fault. I never should've agreed in the first place. But Ollie had guilted me into it, insisting that I never let him take the lead in our schemes.

Which was true.

But there was a good reason why. . . . I was simply *better* at it than he was.

This wasn't an ego thing. It was irrefutable *fact.*

Fact: I was the daughter of the most notorious international thief the past decade had seen.

Fact: I had been the only real partner-in-crime my dad had had since my mom.

Fact: Dad had taught me everything he'd known.

Fact: Now that Dad was in prison for our past heists, I was the only one left to carry on his legacy—minus the whole getting caught part.

True, it was also fact that since coming to live in Greenwich, Connecticut, months ago, I'd taken my now best friend, Ollie, under my wing and begun to teach him the art of thievery.

And while it was also true that we'd already planned and carried out two big jobs together—successfully,

I might add—Ollie was nowhere near my level of expertise yet.

But that was ultimately why I'd agreed to his plan in the end. It was low-stakes stuff. Sure, we could get in trouble if we were caught, but we wouldn't end up in prison or anything.

Well, it was unlikely that we would, anyway.

Still, I felt the need to say something before we got in too deep.

"This isn't going to work," I whispered to Ollie through the dark.

"Shhhh!" Ollie hissed back. "You're going to jinx it, Frankie."

I rolled my eyes even though he couldn't see me do it. Ollie was the kind of guy who believed wholeheartedly in jinxes. And bad omens. And lucky charms. And everything else that I thought was complete hooey.

Yet, he was my best friend.

"Fine," I said between gritted teeth. "I won't . . . *jinx* it. But can I ask just one thing?"

"What?" he asked.

"*Why* are we doing this again?" I asked.

Ollie stopped what he was doing and looked at me, exasperated. "Seriously?" he asked me like the answer was obvious. "Go big or go home, Frankie."

I looked my friend up and down. He was wearing a hot pink, velour track suit and a very long, very blond wig. Besides having naturally full eyelashes, Ollie made for a rather unattractive girl.

"Well, I guess you can't go any bigger than this," I said, giving in to what was about to happen. And how could I not? I'd never seen him so in his element before. So ready for one of our plots. So comfortable taking the lead in a job.

Still, my gut clenched up anyway. Taking a risk like this went against everything I'd ever taught him. It was like, number two on my "things to avoid" list. But I also got why it was necessary. Besides, he was my ride or die. Which meant if he went down, we both went down. And since this was Ollie's show, it would likely be in a blaze of glory.

"Okay," I said, knowing I wasn't going to convince him to call the whole thing off. "I guess we're doing this then."

We went over the plan one last time and then I snuck away, padding quietly down the dark passageway alone. When I finally arrived at a closed door, I paused, noticing the light shining in through the space at the bottom. I watched for a few seconds to make sure there weren't any breaks in the glow, signaling to me that someone was on the other side. There were none.

The coast was clear, so I snuck outside . . .

And into Western Middle School's bustling cafeteria.

Glancing around to make sure I hadn't been spotted

sneaking out from the usually locked backstage area, I was relieved to see that nobody was paying any attention to me.

Just the way I liked it.

I *was* a thief, after all. Being invisible was sort of an important part of my lifestyle. And just because Ollie's end goal was to be seen—by Mrs. Hazel, the school's drama teacher, in particular—it didn't mean it had to be mine.

In keeping with this philosophy, I'd hidden my shockingly white hair underneath a hat and worn ripped, black skinny jeans and a vintage Rolling Stones T-shirt that I'd stolen from my uncle's closet, just to ensure that I didn't stick out like the sore thumb I was.

I might've lived here now for over half a year, but I was still an outsider. I was still sort of the new girl in town, and with the admittedly shocking makeover I'd given myself midyear, I wasn't exactly in line to be voted Most Popular. With the exception of Ollie—who acted like I was the long-lost, bratty sister-from-another-mister he'd never had—nobody seemed to even care that I existed.

And that was fine by me.

Because when you were a master thief—and your uncle (and current guardian) was a cop—laying low was sort of a necessity.

Unfortunately, my bestie held the opposite life goal. And that's ultimately why I was in this mess.

My smart watch vibrated and I looked down to read the text that had come through.

Ready? it read.

"Give me thirty seconds," I spoke back into my watch, and then started to move.

I strolled beside the front of the stage, letting my hand trail along the underside of the platform's edge as I went. Dust and dirt began to build up on my fingertips and I resisted the urge to pull my hand away and wipe it off on my jeans. Because I *needed* to keep my hand there.

A few seconds later, my willingness to get a little dirty paid off.

My fingers touched the smooth plastic mechanism I'd taped out of sight that morning. Without slowing my stride, I pressed the button on the device, heard the faint click, and made a sharp left up the aisle of lunch tables.

I'd only gotten about twenty feet away from the stage, when I heard the large curtains squeaking open behind me, signaling that I had to hurry if I was going to pull off the next part of the plan.

As if on cue, all eyes turned to the stage as Ollie, dressed in the aforementioned head-to-toe pink, stepped to the edge of the platform and began to sing.

"My name is Regina George," Ollie belted out like he was the second coming of Beyoncé. "And I am a *massive* deal—"

It took longer than I'd originally expected for people to realize that the person performing was actually a boy. But once they did, the whispers and pointing began.

I wanted to tell them all to shut up. To give Ollie a chance because he was braver than them all combined. But he didn't need the assist. He was used to standing out. In fact, he'd once told me that if I couldn't find him in the spotlight, then he'd be dying in the shadows.

A bit of a drama queen, that one.

And his performance of "World Burn" from the hit Broadway musical *Mean Girls* was drama with a capital *D*.

Sure, it might've made more sense for him to play the role of Cady's best guy friend, Damian, on account of the fact that he was A) a guy and B) a fantastic sidekick. But Ollie, being, well, Ollie . . . had set his sights on a bigger and juicier part.

That of the Queen Bee herself.

As my friend continued to belt out the words to the song he'd chosen, I made my way toward the faculty's table and stealthily slipped behind Mrs. Hazel.

Most of the adults were watching Ollie with a blend of surprise and amusement as they ate lunches they'd bagged themselves and brought from home. I couldn't see the drama teacher's expression, but she was moving slightly to the beat of the background music accompanying Ollie. That *had* to be a good sign, right?

When Ollie had originally brought up this plan to me, I'd immediately balked. It was too flashy, too risky. How could a plan like this possibly work out in our favor? But

Ollie had insisted it was the only thing that would set him apart from everyone else who was auditioning.

"But it's so obvious!" I'd argued. "Why do you think this stunt will be what gets you the part?"

"Look, maybe you don't understand because you're not a thespian. But Mrs. Hazel is, and she is *absolutely* going to appreciate what I'm trying to do. Actors *crave* drama. The more drama the better. So I'm going to give her drama!"

"That's for sure," I'd muttered to myself. But in the end, I'd agreed to back him up. Because, as he reminded me, he would do the same for me.

Now, as I watched Mrs. Hazel bop around to Ollie's one-man—er, woman—show, I was beginning to think he was right.

I didn't need to see my friend onstage to know what he was doing at any given moment. He'd forced me to watch him perform the song and dance so many times that it was like having a jingle stuck in your head that you couldn't, for the life of you, get rid of.

Which had sort of been his goal since I needed to know exactly when in the song to put the next phase of our plan into motion.

And this happened to be the moment.

I pulled a phone out of my pocket, pressed the first number on the speed dial, and then watched as it connected. Without bringing the phone to my ear, I tossed it into a nearby trashcan, and swung the umbrella I'd been holding this whole time, up into the air and over my head. As I pressed the release, it popped open just as water began to rain down from above.

Kids immediately started to scream all around me as the water soaked their clothes and drenched the remainder of their lunches. Hair that had taken so long to style was ruined and makeup ran down the faces of those who had parents cool enough to let them wear it.

Then, chaos broke out and people began to run from the room, shrieking with equal parts glee and outrage. I gave a little smirk as Annabelle Valera and her minions darted past me, already looking like drowned rats, their perfect country-club-style outfits no longer perfect. Ruining Annabelle's day hadn't been our goal, but it was definitely a pleasant byproduct.

I glanced over at the stage to see if Ollie had witnessed the hilarious takedown of our shared nemesis, but he was still lost in his solo. And I had to hand it to him: the kid was crushing it. Water was dripping down his face like he was standing under a waterfall and he wasn't even flinching.

It brought a whole new level of respect seeing him commit to his role like that, and I gave him a thumbs up as our eyes met. He beamed proudly as he belted out the last few lyrics and then struck a final pose.

I was about to start clapping when I noticed Ollie's gaze drift down from mine. Then his smile faltered. The change was almost imperceptible, but I could tell something was wrong. Only, as far as I'd seen, the whole plan had gone off without a hitch.

Then I followed his eyes downward and immediately knew what had thrown him off.

There, sitting stock-still in her chair, underneath the cover of me and my umbrella, was the drama teacher, Mrs. Hazel.

And she was glaring.

Right.

Up.

At.

Me.

Entry Two

"I can't believe we're not in solitary confinement right now," Ollie breathed as we walked down the hallway and away from Principal Hollycooke's office.

"Don't even joke about that," I warned, pulling off my hat and letting my short, white-blond hair shake free. Originally, chopping off my locks and dying it back to its original color had been an impulsive move backed by a need for rebellion.

Now, I just sort of loved it.

It felt the most like *me* than any of my disguises ever had. And that was saying a lot, considering I'd been *so* many different people over the years, I'd lost count.

"The absolute worst thing in the entire world for someone like me, would be to be locked up," I continued, making a face.

Ollie cringed at my words. "Sorry," he said sheepishly. "My bad bringing up your dad. . . . Hey, that rhymed!"

His face lit up as if he'd just done something incredible, and I almost burst out laughing. But I held it in. Ollie was already soaring pretty high after his little lunchtime performance and I didn't want to give him an even bigger head. If that was possible.

"Clever," I said instead.

"Hey, Ollie! That was the best lunchtime ever!" a girl exclaimed, walking past us.

She didn't even look at me.

"Uh, thanks?" Ollie said, seeming surprised by the compliment. Then he turned back to me. "How is it possible we walked away without being expelled?"

I shrugged.

"There was no evidence," I said simply. "Without that, they have nothing but a hunch. And you can't charge the niece of a local detective with a crime that there's no proof she committed."

"Right!" Ollie said, nodding his head slowly as he caught on. "And there was no evidence because . . ."

He waited for me to finish the sentence for him. So, I obliged.

"Because *whoever* rigged the sprinklers to go off at the precise moment you were giving your performance, must've been smart enough to toss the evidence—an untraceable burner phone—into one of the many trash cans around the school. And it was just luck that I had my umbrella with me today. Like I told Principal Hollycooke, you never know when it'll start to rain."

Ollie shook his head in awe and then said seriously, "Have I ever told you that you're the wind beneath my wings?"

"Oh stop," I said, swatting at him. "You're making me blush."

He wasn't, of course. I had more control over my emotions than that. But I was pleased by the sentiment.

"Yo, Ollie—or should I call you *Olivia*?" a Neanderthal named Toby shouted as he stood by his locker with a few of his friends. "You know, my sister has a frilly little tutu you could borrow sometime if that's your thing."

I rolled my eyes and started to open my mouth to say something, but Ollie beat me to it.

"Oooh, tutu's are totally in this season," Ollie insisted to me. Then he turned back to Toby innocently. "At least *someone* in your family has style."

Toby's stupid grin faded as he processed what Ollie had said and his friends began to laugh at him instead.

"Nice!" I said, holding out my hand for him to slap.

"It was just too easy," Ollie responded, like it was nothing. "So, did Mrs. Hazel seemed impressed at all before—"

At that exact moment, someone ran right into us, knocking the wind out of Ollie and causing me to drop my bag in the process.

"Whoa!" I exclaimed, whirling around to get a look at whoever had tried to tackle us.

But the person I found standing there seemed almost as stunned as we were by the collision.

"Oh my gosh, I am *so* sorry, you guys!" a smallish girl said with a grimace as she fought to regain her balance.

I narrowed my eyes at her, trying to decide whether she'd done it on purpose, but she seemed too flustered for it to have been anything other than an accident. She was dressed in jeans and a faded T-shirt that read MY PATENT IS STILL PENDING. . . . and her dirty blond hair was pulled up into a messy bun on top of her head like she hadn't given her looks a second thought when she'd gotten ready that morning. I watched as she pushed her glasses back into place with a shaky hand before leaning down and retrieving my bag.

"I'm sorry," she said again, handing it back to me. Then, as if recognizing who we were for the first time, she forced a smile. "Oh, hey, Ollie. I heard you performed something at lunch? Some kind of water show?"

"Hey, June," Ollie responded, straightening out the purple shirt he'd changed into after dripping all over the floor of Principal Hollycooke's office. It wasn't as eye-catching as the pink velour number he'd been wearing, but it also wasn't exactly camouflage. "And it was more like a musical number than a Cirque du Soleil show. . . ."

June nodded, though we could both tell she wasn't fully paying attention.

"You okay?" I ventured, feeling like she needed someone to ask her the question. I didn't know her, but it was obvious that something was wrong.

"Yeah," she said absently. Then, all of a sudden, her face crumbled and she looked like she was about to cry. "No. I'm not okay."

Ollie and I looked at each other and then pulled the agitated girl away from the middle of the hallway and into a nearby bathroom. Once we were alone, Ollie locked the door behind us and I reached into my bag for some tissues.

"What's going on, June?" Ollie asked, rubbing her back as it heaved with sobs.

She sniffled loudly and then wiped at her face with the Kleenex.

"Thanks," she said to me, but immediately started to cry again.

"No problem," I said slowly, and then gave Ollie a look that I hoped said, *You know her better than I do. Take point.*

His eyes widened like he understood and then he cleared his throat.

"Girl, you have *got* to take a breath," Ollie said, forcing June to focus on his eyes. "Breathe in. Breathe out. Breathe in. Breathe out. There. Now why are you ugly-crying?"

I shot him a look.

"I mean," Ollie stammered. "Not that you're *ugly*. You know the expression, right? *You* are actually very pretty in an artsy kind of way—"

"Ollie, stop," I commanded, shaking my head.

Boys were never good with crying girls. It was like they panicked because they just didn't know how to deal.

Luckily, I did.

"June, what's wrong?" I asked simply.

She wiped her tear-streaked cheeks with the back of her hand and then took a deep breath.

"It's gone," June said, shakily.

"What's gone?" I asked, my interest already piqued.

"My invention for the Alia Thomas Institute contest," she said as if I was supposed to know what that was.

I looked to Ollie, confused.

"The Alia Thomas Institute is this super-snooty private school about half an hour away," Ollie said. When he saw the O shape that June's mouth morphed into, he backtracked. "I mean, not snooty. *Exclusive*."

"And expensive," June added. "That's why I need to win the contest. It'll give me a spot at the school *and* a scholarship. Otherwise, I can't afford to go."

"But your parents aren't poor," Ollie said without thinking.

I sighed.

Sometimes the fact that my friend didn't have a filter made interactions like this a little touchy.

"That's sort of the problem?" June answered, not at all bothered by Ollie's comment. "My folks make a decent amount from their jobs. Not a ton, but enough that we're *comfortable*, anyway. But that means we don't qualify for financial aid. And I've got four brothers and sisters at home . . ."

She didn't need to finish the sentence for us. We understood that without the school giving her a break on the financial side of things, she wouldn't be attending.

"That sucks," I said, and I meant it. The fact that you

could make too much money to qualify for help, but not enough to actually afford going to a school seemed like a particularly cruel punishment. "But they have a contest to go for free?"

June nodded, her eyes opening wide.

"This is the first year they're doing it," she says, her voice filling with excitement. "They're holding these contests at all the schools in the area to recruit the top performers. The students who show up with the best inventions win admission and a full ride. And graduating from Alia means you can pretty much go to any tech college you want."

"College?" I repeated, surprised to hear someone our age even thinking that far ahead.

I didn't even know what my next heist was going to be, let alone what I'd be doing after *high school.*

"Yeah," she said, giving me a small smile. "I've got my sights set on MIT."

"Well, I doubt that'll be a problem," Ollie said, wandering over to the mirror and studying his reflection absently. "Science and tech is sort of your thing, right? You don't even take classes with us anymore."

I looked at him quizzically.

"Too smart," he explained.

"I take online classes at the high school," she confirmed.

Sheesh.

"Wait," I said, confused. "If you're the female Einstein

and everything, you're obviously going to win. So, what's the problem then?"

June looked up at Ollie and me, her eyes brimming again with tears.

"The problem," she said finally, "is that someone stole my entry."

Entry Three

"Someone took your idea?" Ollie asked, scrunching up his nose in disbelief.

June shook her head. "Someone actually stole *it*," she said. "The invention itself."

"Who would want to take it, though?" I asked her, genuinely curious now. "Are there really that many people entering the contest?"

I hadn't even heard of this Alia Thomas school before, let alone any competition to get into it. Could there really be that many Western MS students who wanted to go to a science and tech school badly enough to steal someone's entry?

And what had June invented that would be worth stealing?

"There are a dozen kids from our school alone who are competing," June said, nodding her head seriously at me.

"I didn't realize there were that many Sci-Hards here," I said, surprised.

"Maybe they just want to escape *this* place," Ollie said with a snort. "Anywhere else will do."

"True, not all the entrants are exactly my competition,"

June confirmed. Then, she looked suddenly sheepish. "Not that I'm saying I'm better than anyone, just, well—"

"You don't have to explain yourself to us," I said, cutting her off. "I'm sure you *are* the best. It's not like Western is a hot spot for super talents or anything."

"Hey!" Ollie exclaimed, making a face at me. "Did you not see my performance this afternoon?"

I rolled my eyes.

"Okay. Present company excluded," I amended.

"That's better," Ollie said, still pouting.

"So, people know that you're the one to beat," I said out loud, starting to pace the floor of the small bathroom. "Who's your competition?"

"What are you thinking, Frankie?" Ollie asked me suspiciously.

But my mind had already begun to hum.

"Um, Gina Oliver, Hayden Cruz, Liam Boneventure, Taylor Shoup, Annabelle Valera, Grace DeWinthrope—"

"We'll get your invention back," I said suddenly, surprising them both by my declaration.

"You will?" June and Ollie asked at the same exact time.

"We will," I answered. Then I turned to June. "And we'll do it *before* the contest begins. When is that, by the way?"

June swallowed hard.

"Tomorrow?" she squeaked.

Crud-buckets.

"Right," I muttered, thinking hard about what this meant. "Of *course* the contest is tomorrow. Because otherwise it would be too easy."

"But we don't even know who took it . . ." June started to say and then let the words trail off.

"I think I do," I said slowly. "And it would be my pleasure to take her down."

"Her?" Ollie asked, not following.

"Her," I repeated.

"Oh, boy," he said, letting out a low whistle. Then a smile broke out across his face. "Or in this case, *girl*."

June looked back and forth between the two of us, as if she was worried we were too good to be true.

We weren't.

We'd gone after bigger ticket items than a middle school gadget. And we'd taken down far shadier characters than our new mark. Heck, in the last six months alone, Ollie and I had robbed a corrupt real estate mogul and a duo of exotic animal traders. And then we'd sent them all to prison.

This was nothing.

Something to pass the time.

Who knows? It might even be fun. Besides, it'd be a good side project to keep my head in the game until we decided what our next big heist would be.

"Um, not that I'm not grateful you're going to try to help," June said, choosing her words carefully, "but have you guys done anything like this before?"

Ollie laughed like it was the joke of the century, while I managed to keep a straight face.

"Well, no," I answered honestly. "We've never done anything like *this* before."

June's face fell.

"But, I've picked up a few things over the years," I continued. Then, as if to explain, I added, "My uncle is a detective with the Greenwich PD."

"Oh!" June exclaimed, relief flooding her face. "Okay. So, what do we do now?"

"You go home and get some rest," I instructed.

"That's it?" she asked in disbelief.

"Yeah," Ollie asked, raising an eyebrow at me. "That's it?"

I shot Ollie a glance that said to relax. When he crossed his arms and took a step back, I turned back to June.

"So, what are we looking for?" I asked, pulling on my bag and making my way to the bathroom door. "A robot? Potato lamp? Or maybe the ever classic erupting volcano?"

"A hard drive," June answered.

"You built a hard drive?" Ollie spat out from behind us.

He might've said it first, but I was just as impressed. Only, it wasn't really an invention if it already existed, right?

"No," June said, laughing for what might've been the

first time since our conversation had started. "My invention is *on* a hard drive."

"Oh," I said, less impressed now. "Okay. So, just an ordinary, everyday hard drive then? Are you sure someone didn't just mistake it for their own?"

"Definitely not," June said. She must've seen the doubt on my face, because she added, "My hard drive is neon green and has a sticker on it that says YOU'RE SODIUM FUNNY. I could be wrong, but I'm pretty sure it's one of a kind."

"Fair enough," I said, pulling the bathroom door open and spilling out into the hallway.

As we began to join the throngs of students walking to their classes, it was hard not to notice the general dishevelment of everyone as they passed by. Like they'd been caught in a downpour. Only . . .

"Is it raining outside?" June asked, perplexed as she seemed to notice everyone else for the first time.

"Nope," I answered, regaining my balance.

"Then why . . ." she started, letting her words trail off as she tried to work out what was happening around us.

"Ollie?" I prompted.

"That," he said, with a grin, "would be my lunchtime performance."

Entry Four

"You two are in deep water," Uncle Scotty said to Ollie and me as he walked through the front door with a bag of tacos for dinner.

"*Technically*, the water wasn't that deep," Ollie said as he twisted side to side on one of our barstools.

My uncle gave him a disapproving glare and unceremoniously dropped the bag onto the counter. It landed with a cracking thud and I couldn't help but wince.

"My hard shells!" Ollie exclaimed, hopping off the chair and running over to the food. Looking inside, he inspected the contents for damage before finally letting out a sigh of relief. Then he began to rummage through the bag like he hadn't eaten in days.

"Broken tacos should be the least of your worries after what you pulled today," Uncle Scotty warned as he crossed his arms seriously. Then he looked over at me, his eyes narrowing slightly. "Pulling the fire alarm? Really, Frankie?"

I threw my hands up in the air like I was fending off the accusation. "I swear I did *not pull the fire alarm*, Uncle Scotty," I said honestly.

"That's true," Ollie said, his mouth already full. "She didn't pull the alarm, Detective."

My uncle made a face as he watched Ollie inhale another taco in just a few bites.

"Would you at least get a plate?" he asked him, sighing. "I *know* you weren't raised in a barn."

"*I* lived in a barn for a while," I said, sauntering over to the table thinking about those months in Portugal with Dad.

Uncle Scotty groaned. "Please don't remind me of my brother's monumental errors in judgment."

As we talked, Ollie reluctantly put down his half-eaten taco and went over to the cabinet. Retrieving a stack of plates, he brought them to the table and lay them out in what had become our normal spots during meals.

When I'd first come to live with Uncle Scotty after Dad had gone away, family dinners had been mandatory. Sort of like our special uncle/niece bonding time.

But it wasn't long before Ollie had become a regular fixture at our house too, preferring to eat with us rather than with his own family. Not because he didn't get along with them. But because he had a full house.

We're talking grandmas and grandpas and aunts and cousins full.

At home he had to fight for attention. At my house, he had no competition. Uncle Scotty and I weren't exactly chatters, so Ollie was free to hold court. In a way, it was a win-win for everyone involved. Ollie had a captive audience in us, and the Lordes just got to sit back and watch. Which was how we liked it.

Except for maybe times like this, when Ollie and I teamed up for a shared goal against Uncle Scotty.

This one being our desire to avoid getting into trouble.

I slipped down into my chair and pulled a burrito from the pile of food, then took a huge bite.

Uncle Scotty was still eyeing us.

"Did neither of you eat lunch?" he asked bluntly.

"Not really," Ollie said, mouth already full again.

"We were sort of . . ." I began before pausing.

How was I supposed to put this in a way that wouldn't get me in trouble?

". . . *busy* during lunch," I finished carefully.

"Flooding your school?" Uncle Scotty asked, sitting down now too.

I rolled my eyes.

"Is that what Principal Hollycooke said?" I asked, annoyed by this. "You got some bad information, Detective. If this were one of your cases, you wouldn't convict me based on hearsay, would you? Come on, we both know you're better than that."

He raised an eyebrow at me and tried to hide a tiny smile before taking a bite of his own taco. He loved it when I showed an interest in his job. Especially when it had to do with being on the right side of the law.

"Okay," he said, conceding this point. "But Frankie, do you really want me to do my own investigation into this? You *know* I'm good."

"Not *that* good," I teased.

"Excuse me?" he asked, feigning shock. "Is that a challenge?"

I shook my head. "Not at all," I answered, my face innocent. "I'm simply saying that you won't find anything tying us to what happened today."

"That's not exactly a denial," Uncle Scotty said frowning.

I gave him a little pout.

"Don't you trust me, Uncle Scotty?" I asked, hoping he did but knowing he shouldn't. At least, not in this case.

He sighed.

"Fine," he agreed, though I could tell he wasn't convinced of our innocence in that day's debauchery. "But if they find any proof that it *was* you two, then you *will* pay for it. Literally. For any damage that was done."

"There wasn't any damage," Ollie spoke up then. "It happened in the cafeteria, so they just had to mop up the water. Which they technically do at the end of every day anyway. So, in a way, they just got a jump on the cleanup."

"You're already skating on thin ice, Ollie," my uncle cautioned. "Do you really want to go there?"

"Bottom line," I jumped in before Ollie could dig both our graves. "Do you honestly think that if *I'd* planned something, that there would be any evidence to find? Come on, you know *I'm* better than that."

It was a subtle reminder of my former life of crime,

yet it spoke volumes. My dad had been one of the best in the biz and he'd taught me everything he knew. Everything *I* knew. And I wasn't exactly in the habit of getting caught.

I watched as Uncle Scotty thought about this. In the end, he must've known there wasn't enough proof of our guilt to punish me, because he just sighed in defeat.

"Anything *else* happen today that I should know about?" he asked finally, opting to change the subject.

Ollie perked up at this.

"I performed an unforgettable rendition of 'World Burn' for the student body," he said, excitedly. "I could do it again for you now if you want!"

Ollie almost fell out of his chair as he scrambled to get up and strike his opening pose. Uncle Scotty's eyes flew open in surprise and he choked a little on his food.

"I think he was talking to me, O," I said, and then held back a laugh after seeing the look on my uncle's face.

"Oh."

Ollie's disappointment radiated from his every pore as he collapsed back into his chair, moping. Then he grumbled barely loudly enough to be heard, "Whatever. I don't have my music with me anyway."

I shot my uncle a look. He sighed.

"Maybe you can show us later? After we've eaten?" he suggested, trying to sound more enthusiastic than he clearly was.

"I'll have to see how I feel," Ollie said, still miffed by

the rejection. "I should probably rest my singing voice anyway since official auditions are tomorrow. Though I don't know why I even have to try out after today. . . ."

Hoping to avoid another lecture from Uncle Scotty, I cleared my throat loudly.

"There actually *was* something else that happened today that was sort of weird," I offered. "Have you heard of the Alia Thomas Institute?"

Uncle Scotty thought for a moment before responding.

"Private school in the area?" he asked. I wasn't sure whether it was a guess or that he'd actually heard of it before. But it didn't matter.

I nodded.

"So, apparently they're holding a contest to find the next big science geek," I explained. "The winners get a full scholarship and entry into their school."

Uncle Scotty looked surprised.

"I didn't know you were interested in science," he said slowly.

Ollie burst out laughing. Only he was in the middle of taking a drink at the time, so soda shot out of his nose.

"I'm not," I said, wiping droplets off my arm as I glared at my friend.

"Yeah," Ollie managed to choke out as he caught his breath. "Science and Frankie *so* don't mix. Get it?"

We both looked at him blankly.

"Like oil and water?" he asked, grinning. "Come on, guys! It's a science joke!"

I shook my head before continuing.

"Anyway," I said, turning back to my uncle. "There's this girl in our class named June and she's some kind of tech wizard. She was a shoo-in to win, but somebody stole her invention."

I watched Uncle Scotty's eyebrow lift with curiosity.

"And the contest is tomorrow," I added, sealing his interest.

He finished chewing and then laced his fingers together like he always did when he was trying to work out a problem.

"Are you sure she didn't just misplace it?" he asked.

Ollie and I share a glance.

"She wouldn't misplace it," I said.

Uncle Scotty looked at me skeptically.

"Alia is her dream," I explained. "Her invention is her ticket in. She's not just setting it down somewhere and forgetting where she put it."

"Hmmm," he said, giving this some thought. "Definitely sounds suspicious. Did she go to the school? Tell them what happened? Maybe if she explains it to the judges of the contest, they can give her an extension?"

I shook my head.

"It's not like they can postpone a contest like this. They've had it set up for months now. I doubt they're going to stop everything just because someone's entry has gone missing. And the school is sort of useless. You've met Principal Hollycooke. Do you really think she's going to launch an investigation into a stolen gadget? Yeah, right. She'd just assume June was another careless kid who'd lost her personal property."

Uncle Scotty's eyes raise at this. He'd clearly caught on to the fact that he'd pretty much thought the same thing just a minute ago. I didn't push the insinuation further.

"Do you have any suspects?" he asked finally, choosing not to take offense to my comment.

"I have a few," I said, even though I would've bet my whole thieves trunk that it was just one person in particular.

He smiled. "Well, somebody once told me that you can't convict someone of a crime without any evidence."

I rolled my eyes.

"So, she should just do . . . *nothing*?" I ask, annoyed. "And the person who stole it just gets away with it? And her whole future is ruined? That's not fair."

Uncle Scotty frowned.

"You're right," he said, simply. "It's not. But there's not much else you can do besides tell the school and let them handle it."

I kept quiet after that. Not because I agreed with my uncle. But because I didn't.

And because I knew that I was the only one who could make it right.

Entry Five

"That's twice today that we've avoided punishment," Ollie said, flopping down onto my bed with a groan. "You really *are* that good, aren't you?"

"Duh," I said, collapsing down beside him, feet resting against my headboard.

After we'd finished eating, Uncle Scotty had announced that he'd left some work at his office and that he'd be back later. So, after saying good night, Ollie and I had dragged ourselves upstairs to my room, feeling like we might both explode from eating too much.

After a few minutes of just lying there, I turned my head to Ollie and gave him a look.

"What?" he asked me.

"Ollie . . . ," I said sweetly, giving him a smile.

"*What*?" he asked again, the dread creeping into his voice.

"We're taking June's case," I announced calmly.

"We're taking *cases* now?" he exclaimed, barely able to roll himself over to look at me.

"No," I answered. "We're just taking *this one*."

"But I have auditions tomorrow," he whined, kicking his legs around like he was throwing a fit. "I need my beauty sleep tonight, Frankie. Regina George does not *do* puffy. I can't be running around all night long, trying to figure out who stole June's project. Not tonight. I mean, if we were taking down a bad guy, I'd be there. . . ."

I sighed and looked up at the ceiling.

"We sort of *are* taking down a bad guy," I argued, though the fight was already leaving me. His bailing was actually fine. One less person I needed to worry about getting caught in the process.

"That's okay," I said. "I'll ride solo on this one."

He looked at me. "You sure?"

I took a breath and let it out. "I think I'll manage," I said sarcastically.

"Where are you going to start?" he asked me, curiously.

"At Annabelle's, of course."

"Of course," Ollie said, unsurprised. "And you think she's got it because . . ."

He let the question hang in the air, waiting for me to answer.

"Because it's *Annabelle*," I answered, like this was the most obvious thing in the world. Then I paused before continuing. "And June might have told me that Annabelle and her squad have been circling her lately. Alluding to the fact that she should bow out of the competition."

"Right," he said slowly. He chewed the inside of his mouth as we lay there, silent again. "And you're going to get her hard drive back, how?"

"Like I always do," I said, forcing myself to sit up. "By stealing it."

• • •

Within fifteen minutes, I'd grabbed my thieving tools, changed my clothes, and was heading out the door.

I didn't even need to sneak out. Uncle Scotty was already gone, having yelled up to us before he'd left to pick something up at the station. The only threat to my plan would be if Uncle Scotty checked on me when he got home. And just in case he did, I'd shut off my lights and stuffed my bed with pillows. Then I'd left my window unlocked and walked right out the front door and into the night air.

I took a deep breath and smiled. It was a good night for a heist.

And an even better night to prove that Annabelle was the snake I've always known she was.

Ollie had agreed that she was the most likely suspect, and for a hot minute, he'd wanted to come along just to have a hand in bringing her down. But his desire to land the lead in the school musical was greater than his need for revenge, and he'd listened to me when I'd told him to go home and go to bed.

"But you'll text me when you're done?" he asked.

"Of course," I'd promised.

It hadn't been hard to find out where Annabelle lived. Her dad, Brooks, was sort of a public guy, considering he was a hedge fund manager and handled most of the town's elite clientele. And of course, they lived on the other side of town. Not in one of the *ridiculously* rich neighborhoods, but they were far from hurting for money.

Annabelle's house wasn't in a gated community, but it *did* have a privacy wall and gate around their property. The rich always thought that a hedge or fence would keep people like me out. But what it really did was give the wealthy a false sense of security.

And it gave me a challenge.

I parked my bike across the street and studied the entrance. There was only one camera that I could see, and it was pointing at the gate. The wall was covered with ivy and free of any other electronics. There was always the possibility that the Valeras had security patrolling the grounds inside, but after ten minutes of surveillance and no sight of anyone walking by the gate, it seemed unlikely.

Good, it would make my job that much easier.

I left my bike hidden in a bush and ran quickly across the street. Without slowing, I took a running leap at the wall and ran up its side, my fingers finding their way around the strands of foliage affixed to the structure. Creeping up the rest of the way, I peeked over the top, and got my first look at where Annabelle called home.

The mansion was sleek, a contemporary behemoth that managed to block out the light shining from the moon just behind it. In the dark, it was all angles and windows, a mixture of wood and metal, making it seem more like a twenty-something bachelor pad than a family home.

In a way the aesthetic fit Annabelle perfectly: it was just as cold and uninviting as she was.

Taking a breath, I pulled myself the rest of the way up the wall and then jumped down onto the grass on the other side, barely making any noise on impact. After taking down the Tiger Twins over the holidays, I'd signed up for parkour classes, figuring it never hurt to have the skills of a ninja.

Well, a ninja warrior, that is.

And one of the first things they taught was how to fall correctly. That's right. There is a right and a wrong way to fall down. The right way leaves you with your bones intact and very little noise to announce your presence.

The wrong way could end in sirens.

Not tonight though, as I unfolded myself from where I had crouched on the ground, and then tiptoed across Annabelle's perfectly manicured lawn. My eyes flitted around as I then sprinted through the shadows, only stopping again once I was flush against the side of the house.

Most of the lights were off inside, except for a few that were shining from the entryway. There was also a faint glow coming from the back of the home and I began to head in that direction to see if anyone was still up.

It was late—after my designated bedtime, at least—but there was always the chance that the Valeras were night owls. Annabelle seemed the type to do whatever she wanted anyway, so it wouldn't surprise me if she decided her own bedtime.

In reality, it didn't matter whether they were awake or not. What mattered more, was knowing where everyone in the house was.

Particularly, where I could enter so I wouldn't be seen.

I kept my head ducked down until I reached a window low enough to see into. When I found one, I took out a compact mirror and slowly held it up in front of me until the kitchen came into view.

A kitchen that was huge.

Shiny steel gleamed from just about every surface and expensive appliances filled every empty space. There was an oversized refrigerator with large glass doors that displayed the contents within. I couldn't help but notice that unlike ours, it was *not* full of half-eaten takeout containers.

The kitchen is usually the heart of every home, but this one was empty. And looked like it was barely used.

My eyes moved over to a set of floor-to-ceiling sliding doors that opened up to the backyard along the rear of the kitchen area. I dismissed it as an option for getting inside almost immediately, but then saw what I'd *actually* been searching for: the alarm system box.

It was too far for me to be able to read what it said on the screen, but I could clearly see the tiny light signaling its armed status. A light that was currently shining a bright, vibrant green.

Green means go.

"I don't mind if I do," I whispered to myself in the dark.

Although it seemed an obvious choice of entry, I did not head straight for the back sliders. Most backyards had lights controlled by motion sensors, and I was not looking for a spotlight to guide my way.

The better option was to find an open window somewhere. Or a side door that I could jimmy open.

I tested the window I was currently hiding under, but it didn't budge. Neither did any of the others on the ground floor. After assessing the rest of the house, I realized that I'd have to set my sights higher.

As in the second story of the house or above.

There were several balconies along the back side of the house. One at the very top that spanned its length, and then two smaller ones on each side down below that.

I pulled off my backpack while keeping my eyes peeled for any movement around me. Then, feeling around inside the sack, I pulled out my trusty grappling hook launcher and studied it fondly. For as many times as I'd used it over the years, it appeared relatively unscathed. The shiny metal prongs that would grip on to just about any surface I wanted them to, were smooth and unblemished.

I ran my hand over the black box that held the electronics for the launcher as well as the gears that would maneuver the ascension rope. Every corner and lever was familiar to me, like an old toy a kid would play with for hours a day growing up.

My dad had never gotten the memo that Play-Dough and action figures were more suitable toys for a five-year-old than a (definitely dangerous if left in the wrong hands) motorized machine that fired four sharp blades at any given target and then delivered the possessor to it in one swift motion.

And yet I'd never gotten a better present in my life. I'd even named her shortly after we'd been introduced. I did not, however, curl up with her before falling asleep at night. She was great company, but the girl would cut you if you weren't careful.

"I've missed you, Miss Spikey," I said quietly as I checked out all her mechanisms to make sure they were still in order. "It's been a minute."

Then I stood up and held her over my head, aiming the claw directly at the railing of the topmost balcony. Miss Spikey weighed in at roughly twenty pounds, but this time when I picked her up, she felt lighter. I wondered if I'd built up the muscles in my arms taking my parkour classes.

"Whoa, Miss Spikey," I said, jokingly. "Have you lost weight?"

I pressed the firing button and pursed my lips as the hook flew through the air and then imbedded itself into the balcony railing. I gave the rope a tug and when I was sure it would hold my weight, I tightened my grip on the handle and hit the switch.

It was so much like flying that for a few seconds, I

forgot why I was there at Annabelle's. What I was there to do. I just simply reveled in the freeing experience.

But before I knew it, the wall of the house was looming in front of me and I was forced to focus again. Once my momentum had come to a stop, I gripped the balcony rail with one hand, and then threw my leg up and over the ledge.

Retracting Miss Spikey's claws from the railing, I gave her a quick pat and then placed her back in my bag. No way was I leaving her behind for Annabelle to find and steal her, too. With her safely tucked away again, I crept over to the first set of doors I saw and pressed my face to the glass.

Inside was dark, with the exception of a sliver of light coming from underneath a door on the other side of the room. I could just barely make out a bed in the dead center of one of the far walls, and after squinting, I was almost positive there were no bodies lying in it. The comforter, while bulky, was flush against the mattress and at least a dozen pillows decorated the head of the bed.

To my delight, nobody had bothered to lock the balcony door, and I slowly turned the handle to let myself inside. The air-conditioning hit my face first, and then came the heavy smell of musky cologne and powdery perfume.

The combo almost made me gag, and I immediately covered both my nose and mouth.

In that moment, two thoughts came to my head:

One: BO would've smelled better than this.

And two: This was not Annabelle's room.

Besides the smell, there was nothing in the room that screamed "a pre-teen girl lives here." There were no frilly touches on the bedding. No posters of international boy band members or collages of friend's photos stuck to a cork board on her wall.

There was no doubt that this was her parent's room.

And thus, it wouldn't be where I'd find June's missing hard drive.

Making my way quietly to the door, I pressed my ear up against it to listen for any signs of life. When nothing came, I snuck out of the bedroom, and down the dark hallway, opening and closing doors as I came upon them.

Just as I was about to give up hope that Annabelle's room was located on this floor at all, I pushed open one final door and immediately stopped in my tracks.

The sweet, candylike scent that followed Annabelle around the school hallways—and which always made me sneeze—gave her away, and I rushed inside, excited to have found her room so quickly.

I let out a breath as the door clicked closed behind me, pausing for my eyes to adjust to the darkness. Just as I was about to move farther inside, a noise that sounded a lot like an angry bear growling, echoed across the room, making me drop quickly to the ground.

Then I almost started laughing.

Because the noise was Annabelle—*snoring*. The prim

and proper and always perfect Annabelle Valera snored! Loudly. Like a garbage disposal.

Getting ahold of myself, I finally tiptoed over to her bed and peered down at her.

The girl's usually smooth and lustrous hair was pulled back in a messy bun on top of her head as she lay there, mouth open wide like she was about to sing. A trail of drool fell down her cheek and added to the wet spot already on her pillowcase.

If the people at Western could see her now.

This gave me an idea. I took out my burner phone and hit record. There was just enough moonlight outside to make it clear that this was none other than my nemesis.

Ollie wasn't going to believe it unless he saw it.

Stifling a laugh, I shoved my phone back into my pocket and began to search around the room. When I finally spied Annabelle's very real Gucci backpack, I hurried over to it and pulled it open. I was just about to rifle through the contents when a voice tore through the darkness, turning my blood cold.

"What do you think you're doing?"

Entry Six

This is probably a good time to mention that I've been caught thieving before. For specific examples, please refer to my first two journals.

Sidenote: This is personal journal number three, in what—unfortunately—is likely to be a series, since my court-appointed therapist feels that journaling is good for the soul. I don't know what writing all my secrets down will do for my *soul*, but it's made for a good record of what I've accomplished since Dad went away. It also makes for great reading material for him, since the prison library only has so many books available to check out at any given time.

Sidenote over.

Anyway, my point is that when I heard Annabelle's voice at my back, I froze. But not because I was scared or didn't know what to do. I froze because I was running through all the options in my head for getting out of my current predicament.

You get caught enough times, you learn to have contingency plans for any foreseeable snafu.

And this was *definitely* a snafu. A snafu of the snobbiest order.

So, what *were* my options?

Option 1: I could make a run for it, fleeing Annabelle's room and escaping back out the way I'd come. I was sure she hadn't seen my face yet and being that I was dressed all in black, there was nothing that would give away my identity. Sure, the cops would likely be called, but I'd be long gone before they got there. The only problem with this plan was that I'd be leaving without the one thing I came there for.

Option 2: I could confront her. Right here, right now. We could finally have it out and I could take my chances that the cops wouldn't be called, considering she'd stolen the hard drive in the first place. I'd be caught, but so would she.

"Don't you dare move, you filthy animal," Annabelle said threateningly before I could decide what to do. "I've got a scrunchie right here!"

"Huh?" I began. But then I realized what she'd said and whirled around in confusion.

When my eyes finally focused on my nemesis in the dark, I abruptly stopped talking. Because Annabelle was exactly where I'd seen her before: sprawled out across her bedspread, snoring away, mouth wide open.

Then, as I watched her, she suddenly called out, "No, please, don't take my phone. I need to use it to call the mouse. He has all the cheese!"

I let out a breath and shook my head. The girl was aggravating even when she was unconscious.

Annabelle sucked in another gulp of air before turning over onto her stomach, and I didn't waste any time getting back to work.

As much as I wouldn't have minded the confrontation, I preferred to have it when I wasn't on her turf.

And with the hard drive in my hand.

I turned back to the Gucci bag, still open, and began to rummage through it.

Lip gloss.

Western MS ID.

Gum.

I cocked my head to the side for a second before pulling out a piece of the gum and shoving it into my mouth. Then I thrust my hand back inside and wiggled my fingers around until they finally closed around something rectangular, metal, and cold. With a smile, I yanked it out triumphantly.

Even in the dark I could make out the sticker that June had mentioned. She'd been right. There was no mistaking her hard drive for someone else's. It was definitely one of a kind.

And it was confirmation that Annabelle had *knowingly* stolen June's invention.

So now she was going to pay.

I threw all her stuff back into the bag and closed it up like I'd found it. Then I began to walk over to the door intending to leave, but suddenly stopped as an idea popped into my head.

Tiptoeing backward until I was standing over her bed again, I zeroed in on her hair, which was still tied up messily on top of her head. I chewed hard on the gum a few times before pulling it out with my fingers.

Then I studied the sticky ball in my hand for a while, before looking slowly back at Annabelle's hair.

And again at the gum.

It wasn't like she didn't deserve it.

But as I debated this particularly cruel move, I spied something else lying next to Annabelle that made me pop the gum back into my mouth.

Putting on my best evil villainess grin, I snatched up the book splayed, words down, on top of the hot pink bedspread. I traced the letters carefully with my gloved finger.

D. I. A. R. Y.

A girl really *should* be more careful with her innermost thoughts and secrets. Like with my journal for instance, I always hid it . . .

Ha! Yeah, right. Like I'm going to tell you.

Although, I guess if you're reading this, then you've already found it. Or somebody has.

Which means I need to find a new hiding spot. . . .

I shook my head to bring my focus back to the matter at hand. Then I shoved Annabelle's diary into my backpack and crept over to her door. A quick peek outside revealed that the hallway was still empty, so I slipped out without making a sound.

I was only steps away from my escape when I heard voices drifting to this part of the house from downstairs. The conversation was low, but not exactly hushed.

After a few seconds, laughter rang out, easy and clear. Even being this far away, I could tell that the sounds weren't coming from just two people.

Looked like the Valeras had company.

Entry Seven

On the one hand, I needed to get out of there. But on the other, my curiosity was piqued.

Satisfied that I could flee anytime I needed to and still not get caught, I decided it wouldn't hurt to get a look at the people who'd created the girl we all knew and loathed.

I made my way down the hallway, past Annabelle's room, to a spot where I could see the light drifting up from downstairs. As I grew closer to the open-style landing at the top of a staircase, I lowered myself down to the ground until I was completely on my stomach. It sounded like I was in the same room now as the people talking downstairs and so I slowly slid my body across the dark, hardwood floor, making sure my movements didn't make a sound that would alert my presence. Once I reached the edge of the landing, I peered down into what I guessed was the home's great room.

And it was, indeed, a *great* room.

If Ollie had been there, he'd probably have described it as crazy great.

There was a huge square coffee table situated right in the middle of the floor, made out of what looked like reclaimed wood, but which probably cost a small fortune. I nearly scrambled backward when I saw flames erupting from the center of it. But when none of the room's occupants were panicking like the house was about to literally go up in smoke, I took a closer look and realized that it was one of those electric fires.

And I had to admit, it was really cool.

Gathered around the indoor fire table were four people. Two men and two women. They were each relaxing on enormous, white, tufted armchairs, the backs of which extended up at least six feet. It gave the illusion that they were holding court in a kingdom somewhere that no longer existed.

"Where's the wife tonight, Brooks?" one of the men asked before lifting a glass full of amber liquid to his lips. Then those lips curled into a smile that could've blinded anyone in the vicinity, as his shockingly white teeth were so straight and perfect I wouldn't have been surprised if he were in toothpaste commercials.

"Oh, she's out with her *girlfriends*." Annabelle's dad waved his hand in the air like this was a regular occurrence.

"And *we* weren't invited?" one of the women asked, feigning shock as she held her hand to her chest dramatically.

The woman was pretty—in a more masculine way—her face all cheekbones and harsh lines. Her dark hair was cut into a curt lob, and the smart glasses she wore on her face didn't extend far enough to hide her thick, yet perfectly shaped eyebrows. She gave off an air of superiority, especially when she let out a loud cackle.

"Oh, come on, Lily," Brooks said, rolling his eyes. "Like *you* would ever be caught dead with that crowd."

The woman named Lily raised an eyebrow and took a sip from her glass. After she swallowed, she touched a delicate finger to the corner of her mouth as if to wipe away a drop of the liquid. Then she smiled at the others, as innocently as she could.

"The last time I talked to Arabella and her friends was at your fundraising benefit, and I swear it was like my brain was oozing out of my ears," Lily said with a snort.

"Well, Arabella's my favorite so far of all your wives," the white-toothed man said with a smirk. "She definitely makes *you* look better, Brooks."

"Oh, ha, ha," Brooks returned, but didn't seem upset by the dig.

"She's always been nice to me," the other woman said, her voice quiet and thoughtful.

This guest was also pretty, but in a completely different way than Lily. Where Lily's body was thin and sharp, this woman was svelte, her limbs extending much longer than seemed should be possible. She had auburn hair that fell down around her shoulders in loose waves and pretty almond-shaped eyes that reminded me of Bambi.

"That's just because she qualifies as half your

business!" Brooks said jokingly. "Great job on her lips this month, by the way, Connie. I keep telling her they're fine the way they are, but she insists on going bigger. And who am I to tell her no?"

He shrugged, though he clearly wasn't broken up over the fact.

"Take it from me, if a woman wants to go bigger, you always say 'yes!'," the other guy said, flashing his smile again. He looked so familiar to me, but I was sure I hadn't met him before.

I feel like I would've remembered him.

"Fair enough, Dakota," Brooks said, grinning back. "I'll shut up from now on."

"Is that a promise?" the other guy baited.

"Ugh. You're both disgusting pigs," Lily said, sighing, and then turning back to Connie. "Can you *believe* we're both still friends with them? Connie? *Earth to Connie*."

The plastic surgeon seemed to snap out of her daze then and forced herself back to the current conversation. But it was clear she'd missed half of what had been said.

"What?" Connie asked distractedly. Then she seemed to catch up. "Oh, right. Yeah. Pigs. Both of them."

Lily's eyebrow raised as she studied her friend.

"Everything okay, Con?" she asked. I got the feeling that the question wasn't one of friendly concern. More like she was fishing for dirt.

Connie let out a deep breath and rubbed at her eyes before picking up and draining the rest of the dark liquid from her fancy, crystal glass. Then she forced a smile.

"I'm fine," she said finally, though not at all believable. "I'm just tired. You know, working long hours and all."

"You should take a vacation with the fam," Lily said, pointing at her like this was the answer to all life's problems. "You definitely deserve it with how hard you work."

Connie just nodded her head noncommittally.

Ugh. I hated it when rich people patted themselves on the back for just existing. Like when someone rewarded themselves with a piece of cake at the end of the day when all they'd done was lay out by the pool and update their social media.

It was maddening.

I started to slide back across the floor, satisfied that I wasn't going to hear anything at all interesting by eavesdropping on these four. As I was trying not to make any noise, Connie began to speak again.

"Yeah, maybe," she said. Then, almost feverishly, she added, "Um, so can we talk about why we're here? It's about the kids, right?"

I stopped sliding and waited for someone to answer. Finally, a throat was cleared and I could hear a glass being set down on a hard surface.

"Sure," Brooks said, his voice taking on a more businesslike tone. "So, I wanted to meet tonight to talk about schools. Specifically, how we're going to get our kids into the schools we *want* them to be in."

I slowly started to soundlessly slide my body back to

the overlook until I could once again see the foursome. At some point Brooks had stood up and had begun to pace around the room.

"And what schools are those?" Lily asked, her eyebrow raised. "Because—and no offense—our kids couldn't *be* any more different. I highly doubt they'll be attending the same institutions."

"What schools? Well, any schools we want, of course," Brooks answered as if this were obvious. Then he added, as if it were an explanation, "Look, Annabelle is trying to score entry into Alia with some contest they're holding tomorrow. But let's be honest: there's no way she's going to win. She's not *that* smart. Clever, but not exactly brainy. Not like her stepsister anyway."

"Where did Clara get her intelligence from anyway? She couldn't have possibly gotten it from her mom," Dakota joked and then snorted.

"Hey, that's my wife you're talking about," Annabelle's dad said, though he didn't seem at all upset by the comment. "Anyways, my point is that Annie's not getting in unless I make it happen. And I know you all are in similar boats."

"Science isn't exactly my kid's thing," Lily said, taking another sip of her drink. "To be honest, I'm not sure he has a *thing*. He's just so *quiet*. Completely different from his brother, thank gosh."

Lily involuntarily winced as she mentioned her older son and avoided the other's obvious glances. Then she took another gulp of her drink and shook her head.

"On second thought, having a little help in the admissions side of things might not be a bad idea," Lily said, still not looking at anyone.

"Cassius sure blew through all the schools in the area, didn't he?" Dakota said with a chuckle.

Even in the darkened light of the room I could see Lily flush.

"Just wait until *yours* hits high school," Lily snapped back. "We'll see if you're still laughing then."

Dakota put his hands up in surrender but didn't wipe the slightly smug smile on his face.

"Sammy has her sights set on a performing arts school," Connie cut in, staring out the floor-to-ceiling windows. I was sure she couldn't see anything outside, but she squinted for a brief second before turning back to the others. "She won't have a problem getting in. The girl has talents I certainly never had."

"I have to agree," Dakota chimed in. "I'd say she should audition for my next movie, but the flick isn't exactly suitable for kids, if you know what I mean."

"No offense, but I don't want her quitting school to become an actress just yet," Connie said, refilling her wine glass. After taking another big drink, she added, "She can be a star *after* she's gotten her degree."

Dakota shrugged. "Hey, if London could go pro now, I'd pull him out of school so fast, you wouldn't see anything except a blur as he disappeared."

"No kid goes pro at his age," Brooks said, rolling his eyes.

"Says who?" Dakota said. "I can make just about anything happen."

"Just because you're *faaaamous*?" Lily singsonged.

"Hey, it doesn't hurt," Dakota responded unapologetically.

"So why isn't he at one of the big athletic schools right now then?" Brooks goaded with a mocking look.

"I said I can make *almost* anything happen," the Hollywood guy said between clenched teeth. It was easy to see he was not used to being told no. And the fact that his kid didn't already have an athletic scholarship seemed to be a point of contention for him. "Apparently a few of the deans aren't *fans* of mine. Not everyone has taste."

"So, there you go!" Brooks said, clapping his hands together. "We all want our kids to succeed, and we could use a little help making that happen."

"And what are you proposing exactly?" Connie asked, skeptically.

Brooks looked at each of them individually, a huge grin on his face.

"We cheat the system," he said, shrugging.

"I like it already," Dakota said enthusiastically.

"But *how* are we supposed to do that?" Lily asked, sounding more curious than against the idea.

"Let's just say I know a guy," Brooks said. "And his name is Mr. Admissions."

Entry Eight

"Mr. Admissions? Really? What kind of name is that?" Ollie asked, making a face as I told him about the previous night's after-hours activities while we walked to school the next morning.

"One that's a little *too* on the nose if you ask me," I responded, gripping the straps of my bag as I walked beside Ollie. "People are so lazy with their pseudonyms lately."

Uncle Scotty had dropped us off a few blocks away from school—a regular habit of ours ever since I'd managed to convince him that having a cop deliver me to the front steps in the morning would definitely ruin my street cred.

Nobody wanted to be friends with a possible narc.

Not that I actually *cared* whether I was friends with any of the other kids at school—though, this was something I'd never reveal to my uncle. I had Ollie as a friend and he was more than enough for me. As far as I was concerned, with friendship, it was quality over quantity all the way.

And despite how goofy and sometimes over-the-top Ollie was, there was nobody more loyal, caring, or honest than him.

Who needed anyone else when you had someone like that?

I looked over at my bestie as we walked along the sidewalk to school, and smiled.

"What?" Ollie asked me. "Why are you smiling?"

"It's nothing," I said, still grinning as we both walked in step up the path toward the auditorium. "I just . . . appreciate that we both think alike."

Ollie seemed relieved by my answer and then returned my smile.

"We don't *totally* think alike," he corrected. "You still won't admit that *The Real Housewives* is the best thing that ever happened to television."

I frowned.

"You're right," I said, deadpan. "We're *completely* different. I'm not sure what I was thinking."

We walked a bit of the way in silence as we passed a group of kids heading in the opposite direction. Once we were out of earshot, Ollie glanced sideways at me.

"So, what's the plan?" he asked me, rubbing his hands together to try and warm them up in the cold morning air. The East Coast was no joke in the wintertime. Dad and I had always gone south for the winter.

As in South America.

"Well, first we go and meet June in the gym to deliver the hard drive to her in time for the contest," I said with a nod.

"Yeah, I'm aware of *that* part," he said, huffing beside

me as he tried to keep up. "I was talking more about this whole Mr. Admissions thing."

"Oh," I said, surprised by this. "Um, there is no plan."

"Now . . . ," he prompted, letting the word linger in the air between us.

"No," I answered, shrugging. "There's no *plan*. Period."

"Really?" Ollie asked, looking incredulous.

"Really," I said. When he continued to stare at me, I sighed and explained further. "Look, am I mad that Annabelle's dad and his friends want to try to get their kids into schools through backdoor channels? Sure. It's not fair. But rich people have been using their money and power to get their undeserving offspring into places for decades. Why do you think there are so many buildings named after wealthy families at all the big universities? It's because people gave major donations to get their kids in."

"And that doesn't bother you?" Ollie asked.

"Of *course* it does," I said. "But what am I supposed to do about it? Take down every person who thinks they can use their money to get what they want? There's not enough time in the world. Besides, I've got bigger fish to fry."

"Like who?" Ollie asked skeptically as we reached the double doors that led to the gym where the Alia contest was conveniently being held.

I grabbed the door handle and swung it open wide.

"Like, *real* evil," I said, tossing my head back and charging into the room.

• • •

It wasn't hard to find June. I just had to look for the girl pacing around in front of a nearly empty table, looking like she'd lost her puppy.

When June's gaze finally landed on Ollie and me, she practically tripped over her own two feet trying to get to us. I motioned for her to stay where she was and hurried over to her booth.

"I didn't think you were coming!" she said breathlessly once we were standing in front of her. Then her eyes widened as she noticed that our hands were empty. "Oh, no. You couldn't get it back."

Her face immediately began to fall, followed by her whole body, like she was deflating right before our eyes.

"Calm down, June," I said quickly, not wanting her to get any more worked up. Then, I placed both my hands on her shoulders and forced her to look me in the eye. "We got it."

"You did?" she whispered, like she didn't believe me.

When I nodded, June's knees buckled like she was going to pass out, and suddenly I was glad I was holding on to her.

"Whoa!" I said, pulling her back up and trying my best to keep her on her feet. "Uh, Ollie? A little help, here?"

But instead of going around the table to steady June, I

felt him suddenly tug on the opening of my backpack and pull something out.

"Here you go," he said triumphantly as he handed the hard drive over. "One invention, returned to its rightful owner."

"Omigod thankyouthankyouthankyou!" she squealed, all her words stringing together like they were one.

"Yeah," I said, shooting Ollie an annoyed look. "Thanks, *Ollie*."

"Oh, it's nothing," Ollie said, waving his hand.

"Seriously, you guys saved my life today!" she said, looking at the piece of machinery in her hands like it was the Holy Grail. "You have no idea."

"Well, we were glad to help," Ollie offered as an alarm went off on his phone. He silenced it before turning back to us.

"Gotta make like a tree," he said.

"Huh?" June asked, looking at him confused now.

"And leaf," he finished. "Make like a tree and leaf? Get it?"

It was like a light bulb went off above our quirky classmate's head and she began to laugh nervously.

"Oh, right," she said, distracted. "Sorry, I'm sort of . . . out of it? I barely slept last night. What, with my whole future hanging in the balance and all."

"Well, hopefully you'll sleep better after you win this thing," I suggested, patting her on the back.

"I hope so," she added, sounding unsure.

"Speaking of winning . . . ," Ollie started. Then I felt him slip his arm into mine before bumping our hips together. "You ready? My audition starts in five."

"Why don't you go ahead?" I asked, looking around until my eyes settled on a booth set up in a far corner. Behind it stood a tall brunette with shining hair and a dazzling smile.

Obviously not *everyone* lost sleep last night.

"I'm going to hang here and watch June take gold," I said, my voice steady and confident.

"Really?" June asked, sounding surprised. Then she lunged at me and pulled me into a tight hug.

"Really," I agreed, giving her a little laugh. She seemed so grateful to have somebody there for her, rooting her on.

Ollie cocked his head to the side and studied me before finally shrugging. "Auditions are probably closed anyway," he said, turning his back to us with a flourish. "Next time you see me, I'll be a Mean Girl."

"Aren't you already?" I teased.

"You would know," he answered back before turning around and walking away.

We watched him as he went, the pep in his step so utterly Ollie that I had to laugh.

"Mean Girl?" June asked, confused.

I shook my head. "It's nothing," I insisted.

The lights overhead blinked on and off once, twice, and a third time before remaining on in all their florescent glory.

"Guess it's time?" I asked June, seeing the panic cross her face.

"I've gotta get ready!" she yelped, suddenly moving around her booth quickly and purposefully.

June dug into her bag for a computer and then placed it out onto the tabletop, thrusting it open and beginning to type like a mad woman. Then, just as quickly, she took out a cable, plugging one side into the computer and the other into her newly reclaimed hard drive. She watched something on the screen and then began to type again, the stress on her face clearly giving way to relief.

"Anything I can do?" I offered, sneaking another glance over at Annabelle's booth.

This time Annabelle was staring back at me and June, a scowl on her pretty little face.

She knew.

I smiled back at her and gave her a little wave.

Good.

"You've already helped so much, Frankie," June said, her words bringing me back. Once I turned to look at her again, I could see that she'd brandished a phone out of nowhere and plugged it into another cable "Seriously, if I win this and the scholarship, it's going to be because of you. How can I possibly pay you back? I don't have a lot of money, but I could maybe take on some babysitting jobs—"

I held up my hand and gave her a genuine smile.

"You don't need to do anything," I said. "Just beat

Annabelle, okay? That will be more than enough thanks for me."

"Annabelle?" June asked slowly. "So, it *was* her."

It sounded like I'd just confirmed what she'd been thinking all along, so I wasn't sure why she was frowning.

"Who else would it have been?" I asked, like there had ever only been one possible culprit.

June shrugged.

"Honestly?" she asked, pained. "It could've been any of them."

She gestured to the booths on either side of her.

"Everyone here wants this as much as I do," she said. "Some might even want it *more* if that's possible."

June gazed around at all the competitors who were putting the final touches on their contest entries, but my eyes were trained on Annabelle.

And hers were locked on the hard drive that was lying on top of June's table.

Entry Nine

"Ah, June Langer!" a man with a tidy little mustache and a baseball cap on top of his head exclaimed as he and a few other adults walked up to June's booth thirty minutes later. It was clear that they were the Alia judges, even without reading the name tags affixed to their chests.

"Mr. Morris," June said, placing her hand in his and pumping it formally. "Good to see you again."

"And you as well," the man in the cap said with a smile.

I couldn't help but think he looked more like a Little League coach than a science geek, but what did I know? Most people would've said I didn't exactly look like their idea of an international thief either.

Who people are on the outside doesn't always reflect what's on the inside. I knew that better than anyone.

"I was excited to read your proposal back in September," Mr. Morris said as he glanced sideways at his colleagues. They all nodded their heads in agreement. "Can't wait to see if you were able to pull it off."

"You won't be disappointed, sir," June said, though her voice was shaking slightly.

I'd moved away from June's table when the judges had appeared and took up a spot out of the way. I was sure June wouldn't even notice that I was gone, considering the excitement of the contest. But now, her eyes searched around for me and there was a nervous look in them.

I gave her a discreet thumbs up when they locked on mine.

This seemed to perk her up and she suddenly stood straighter and began to speak to those crowded around her with a renewed vigor.

"In the past, facial recognition was primarily used by the government to help identify suspects in moments of crisis," June said, turning her computer to face the men and women in front of her. The screen showed examples of how law enforcement, as well as those in national security, were able to find criminals in crowds using software available to them.

The image changed to one of a teenage girl taking a picture of a cute guy. He was grinning at her, a flirty smile on his face. She looked smitten as she snapped the picture.

Then, another picture popped up and replaced the first.

This one showed the girl holding up her cell phone so the screen was visible to us. The top of the screen read WHO'STHAT?, and underneath was a collage of pictures—all of the same guy she'd been taking a picture of in the last frame. Only, the photos weren't just from that day. They were obviously taken on multiple occasions and in different places.

Underneath the photos were details about the guy: his name, where he lived, his likes, dislikes, and a bunch of other random information.

It was like we were looking at a Wikipedia page on an average kid.

Only, that couldn't have been it. No way June thought that another social media app was groundbreaking enough to win a tech contest. The ones that were already on the market were plenty if you asked me. So, what was this Who'sThat? app that she believed would be enough to impress the Alia guys?

Luckily, June was already answering my question.

"My new app, called Who'sThat?, blends social media and facial recognition to create a whole new kind of search engine," June explained. "With it, the user can take a picture of literally anyone and upload it to the app. Then the app will scour the Internet for any articles or social media profiles on the person, delivering a summary of who the person is."

"Interesting," Mr. Morris said, nodding as he seemed to think about what she'd said.

"It's like Shazam but instead of music, it's for people!" I exclaimed.

I didn't even realize I'd said it out loud until the judges and a few others glanced back at me.

"What?" I asked, worried I'd somehow gotten my lines crossed. "Am I wrong?"

June shook her head. "Nope. You're totally right," she said proudly. Then, as if to herself, she added, "That's how I should market it."

One of the judges cleared his throat and June was startled out of her thoughts.

"Sorry," she apologized. "Mr. Morris, you were in the middle of saying something?"

He grinned, enjoying the lively conversation around him, but then continued. "So, I could take a picture of, say . . ."

He looked around the room and after a few seconds, pointed to a man in the corner who was tying off a trash bag and then loading it into a bigger bin he was pushing.

"That guy," he finished, and then set his expectant eyes back on June. "And your app would tell me who he is?"

June gave a genuine smile, no longer appearing hesitant or nervous at all. Then, like a magician, she pulled a cell phone out of what seemed like thin air and handed it over to him.

"Why don't you find out for yourself?" she said, a glint of excitement in her eyes.

He took it and looked at the screen briefly. The app must've already been downloaded onto the phone, because Mr. Morris touched the screen, then walked halfway across the room with it, closed his eyes and then took a picture at random. When he finally reached the booth again, he held up the phone to show the other judges the photo he'd taken of one of Western's janitors.

"And now just press the button that says Who'sThat?, and in seconds you'll have everything you ever wanted to know about . . . er, that guy," June said, pointing to the picture on the phone.

"Okay," Mr. Morris said, and then ceremoniously pushed the button on June's cell phone. Within a few seconds, his mouth started to open up in awe and his eyes grew wide as the app generated the information for him.

"Mr. Morris?" one of the judges asked when he hadn't said anything for quite a while. "Everything all right? Did it work?"

Mr. Morris blinked a few times before turning his attention back to his colleagues.

"Um, yes," he said, sounding a bit dazed. Then, as if a fog cleared around him, he swallowed hard and then shook his head. "I'm sorry, I think we need to . . . go now."

June gave him a confused look. So did everyone else.

"Okay," she said carefully, the disappointment creeping into her voice. "But, do you mind me asking . . . is anything wrong? It was working before. If there's a glitch, I'm sure I could fix it."

June's face scrunched up like she couldn't believe her invention was malfunctioning. And right *now*, of all times.

But looking at Mr. Morris's face, I got the feeling that this was something more than a simple problem with the app. It was as if the judge had been frozen in place, his mouth set in a small O shape, while the rest of him hadn't moved in more than a minute.

Except for his eyes.

Mr. Morris's eyes were darting from one side of the room to the other, and then back down at the phone he held tightly in his hand. So tightly, in fact, that his knuckles had gone white.

These were all very clear body language signs that I'd seen before.

He was nervous. Maybe even scared?

But why?

"Mr. Morris?" June tried again, finally managing to get through to the man. I watched as he blinked a few more times and then forced himself to act normal. The key word here being *act*, because he wasn't fooling me.

"Ah, y-yes, sorry June," he stuttered before spreading his mouth into a pained smile. "Your entry is fine. Well, quite impressive, actually. I'd just like to, um, show some other colleagues if you don't mind? In the meantime, I feel rather confident saying that you have certainly earned yourself a full scholarship to Alia. Congratulations, Miss Langer."

He said this all in one breath, like he was quickly running out of air. He seemed almost fidgety now, as if he had somewhere to be. Or rather, somewhere he needed to run off to.

June's eyes grew wide with surprise as his words sank in and then slowly changed to confusion, like maybe she hadn't heard him right.

"Wait—I *won*?" June asked in disbelief.

The other judges were looking at one another as if they were wondering the same thing but didn't find it appropriate to ask out loud.

"Yes, Miss Langer. You've won. We'll be contacting you soon to work out the details," he said, distracted again. Then he held up June's phone. "Might I return this to you at a later date?"

June blinked. "Yes," she said quickly. "Yes, of course. You can have it. It's a disposable."

Then, without saying anything else, Mr. Morris abruptly walked away leaving everyone to stare after him.

I hurried over to June, who was looking around for some kind of an explanation.

"What just happened?" she asked me as soon as I was by her side.

"I was just going to ask you the same thing," I said. "Were you the last entrant? Or did he just . . . leave in the middle of the contest?"

"I don't think I was last," she said, glancing at the booth across from her. "Henry hasn't even gone yet. And he created a recycling robot."

"Seriously?" I asked, raising an eyebrow.

"I mean, it's a robot that can crush soda cans, but it's still pretty cool," she said with a shrug.

I pulled our focus back to her win.

"Was your app really a hypnotizing device?" I said jokingly. "Because he started acting like a zombie after he pressed that button."

"I know," she said. "But it definitely didn't have hypnotizing capabilities—although *that* would be a cool invention."

June got a far-off look on her face as she mulled this over. Then, without any warning, she did a little celebration jump, propelling both of her arms into the air in victory.

"I won!" she exclaimed excitedly before giving me a hug.

I returned it with a little laugh, but as I pulled away, one thought crept into my head.

What did Mr. Morris see on that screen that had him running so scared?

Entry Ten

I was deciding between a slice of pizza or a taco boat, when I felt someone come up behind me. One of my biggest pet peeves was when people felt like it was appropriate to stand super close to me—especially strangers. Probably because I knew from years of experience that the closer you were to someone, the easier it was to steal from them. Needless to say, I had no problem telling someone to back off when they weren't respecting my personal space.

I was about to do just that when a voice whispered in my ear.

"Don't hate me because you're jealous."

I let out the breath I'd been reserving for whoever was creeping up on me once I recognized the voice.

"So, you got the part?" I asked, going back to trying to decide what I wanted to eat for lunch.

Ollie appeared by my side.

"I got *a* part," he responded, jutting out his chin in annoyance.

"Well, that's good, right?" I asked, watching the people in front of us move to the checkout area. "I mean, it sort of *was* a long shot to go for a female role, wasn't it?"

"Long shot?" Ollie asked, tilting his head to the side like maybe he hadn't heard me right.

"Well, yeah," I said with a shrug. "I figured it'd be a stretch for a school in *this town* to allow a boy to play a girl's role in the school play. But you'll definitely crush it as Damien."

Ollie crossed his arms over his chest like I'd said something offensive.

"Oh, I *got* a girl's part," he responded, seeming annoyed now.

I blinked.

"That's amazing, Ollie! I knew you could do it!" I said, stepping forward to congratulate him.

"Knew you could do what?" a girl said, suddenly beside us.

I jumped at the sound.

"Geez, you guys should wear bells," I muttered.

"Hey, June," Ollie said, looking over my shoulder at her. "I was just telling Frankie that I got the role of Gretchen in the musical."

June made a face.

"Oooh," she said, sucking in air through her teeth. "Sorry about that, Ollie. I know you wanted Regina. What a bummer."

I looked back and forth between the two of them.

"What's wrong with playing Gretchen?" I asked, confused. "She's a Mean Girl too, right?"

They both stared at me a second like I'd just said something crazy.

"And next you'll be telling me that green M&M's taste the same as the other M&M's," Ollie said, his eyebrow raised.

I remained silent.

"Omigosh, Frankie!" Ollie said, throwing his hands in the air and then bringing them down his face in exasperation. "How are we even friends!"

"Well, now I feel bad raining all over your parade with my good news," June said to Ollie, looking sheepish.

He waved his hand in the air at her.

"Go for it," he said gloomily. "My day couldn't possibly get any worse."

"*June Langer*!" an angry shriek rang out through what seemed like the whole cafeteria.

"I stand corrected," Ollie said without missing a beat.

"Uh, hi, Annabelle," June said, frowning as the pretty brunette marched up to us. I looked around and saw that nearly the whole student body had turned to watch, too.

"How did you get it back?" Annabelle hissed, stomping her foot in obvious irritation. "Did you seriously break into my house?"

"*What*?" June exclaimed, perplexed.

"Don't play dumb," Annabelle said, rolling her eyes. "We both know you're not."

"Oh, well, uh, thanks?" June said, unsure what was happening.

"It wasn't a compliment," Annabelle said, placing her hands on her hips.

"It kind of was," Ollie pointed out. "You said she was smart."

"Ugh!" Annabelle practically screamed in frustration. "You guys are the worst!"

"Are we smart or are we the worst?" I asked with mock seriousness. "You *really* need to make up your mind, Annabelle."

This seemed to put her over the edge because suddenly her eyes were like two balls of fire and they were trained on the three of us.

"You broke—into—my house—and took—the hard drive—" Annabelle said, breaking up the sentence because she was breathing so hard with anger.

I raised up a hand to interject.

"Not *a* hard drive," I pointed out. "*June's* hard drive."

"And then you brainwashed the judges or blackmailed them or did something shady to make them choose *you* as the winner—" Annabelle continued through clenched teeth.

"Wait, you won?" Ollie exclaimed as he turned to June with delight on his face. "That's stellar, June! Why didn't you say something? Did you know she won, Frankie?"

June beamed at us sheepishly.

"I was just about to tell you when Annabelle—" June started to say, but then saw the look on the other girl's face and stopped midsentence.

"When Annabelle so *rudely* interrupted?" I finished, crossing my arms.

"Excuse me?" Annabelle said, furious as she tried to keep up with our conversation.

"Well, it *was* rude," Ollie declared.

Annabelle whirled on him.

"Why are you even speaking?" she said. "Aren't sidekicks supposed to be seen and not heard? There's a reason Mrs. Hazel gave you the part of Gretchen. You were only ever meant to live in my shadow. And apparently, Frankie's, too."

Ollie's face dropped and I knew that she'd managed to get to him.

"Well, the only reason you got the part of Regina is because you're practically her twin," Ollie shot back. "Except *she's* prettier."

"Whatever. Point is, I won and you lost," Annabelle said, putting her hands on her hips. Then she turned back to June. "Which is what should have happened this morning."

"What happened this morning," I cut in forcefully, "is that June won the contest fair and square, even *after* you stole her invention."

Annabelle's head whipped around and she narrowed her eyes at me. "You have no proof it was me," she bit back.

"Yes. I. Do.," I said, slowly so she'd really understand me.

"How?" she challenged, still sure that she had the upper hand.

I leaned in toward her now like I was about to tell her a secret.

"Because," I said quietly, "I stole it back."

Annabelle let out a little gasp at this, and when I pulled away from her, she looked angrier than I'd ever seen her.

"I should've known it was you, Lorde," she spat. "You've been trouble ever since you got here. You know, maybe I should tell the cops what you've been up to."

I took a sharp intake of breath.

"You want to play *that* game?" I asked, standing up a little straighter now.

"You know I do," Annabelle taunted.

"Uh-oh," Ollie said out of the corner of his mouth as he leaned in toward June. "This is not going to end well."

"Should we get someone?" June asked.

"For *her*," Ollie clarified. "This isn't going to end well for *Annabelle*."

"Oh," June said slowly, her eyes widening. "Okay."

"Fine," I said, forcing my anger down so I at least appeared calmer than I felt. People always made mistakes when they were mad. And I didn't want to mess this up. "You tell the cops—one of which is my uncle, by the way—that we took June's invention back, and we'll tell them that you *stole* it in the first place."

"You broke into my house," Annabelle accused.

"I retrieved a stolen invention from *your* school bag," I corrected.

"Which was in my *house*," Annabelle said between clenched teeth.

I rolled my eyes. "Do you really think that anyone's going to believe that a middle schooler broke into your house?" I said, like it was the wildest thing I'd ever heard. Then I paused. "Actually, it's kind of a compliment that you believe I'm smart enough to pull off something like that. So, thanks, Annabelle. I never knew you thought so highly of me. . . ."

I let my words trail off, smiling at the angry girl standing in front of me. Then Annabelle lowered her voice and squinted at me as what I said sunk in.

"I think *nothing* of you," she hissed through gritted teeth. "In fact, I try not to think of you at all. But I also *know* you were behind this. And just for that, I'm going to make it my mission to destroy you—and any of your lame friends. So, Watch. Your. Back."

As she said these last words, she poked me in the arm.

I wanted to shove her finger back at her, but instead I just chuckled.

"You think I'm scared of you, Annabelle?" I said, standing up straighter. "It's *you* who should be scared of me."

"And why should I?" she said, suddenly playing bored. "I always get my way in the end."

I took a step toward her and noticed that she leaned back just the tiniest bit.

She was intimidated by me.

"Not this time," I said.

Then, without waiting for a response, I motioned to Ollie and June, and we left Annabelle standing there staring after us.

Entry Eleven

The three of us didn't say anything to one another as we filed out of the cafeteria. The silence didn't last long though, and as soon as we took a step outside, the questions started to come.

And it was all at once.

"Did you really break into Annabelle's house to get my project?" June asked at the exact same time that Ollie said, "You realize you just started a war, right?"

Without answering either of them, I said, "Well that was . . . a *treat*."

Ollie snorted and then sashayed ahead before turning to face us again, showing off his skills as he walked backward. As clumsy as he was sometimes, he never missed a step when he was pretending to walk a catwalk, which he was doing right now. It was actually quite impressive, and as I watched him, I almost forgot what I'd just done.

Almost.

Because they were both right. Annabelle knew I'd broken into her house, *and* I'd officially started an all-out war. Not my finest moment, I admit. But go big or go home, right?

Ollie didn't bother waiting for me to answer him, he just pushed forward with the inquisition.

"What did you expect her to do after you . . . *did what you did*," Ollie said to me, emphasizing the last part loudly. And in case I wasn't able to crack his not-so-subtle code, he wriggled his eyebrows mischievously at me and jerked his gaze over to June.

"So, you *did* break in." June breathed quietly and looked at me as if in awe.

"Smooth," I said to Ollie flatly. "Way to be stealth."

Ollie held up his hands questioningly. "What?" he asked. "Hey, at least I didn't flat-out *tell* Annabelle."

"I can't believe you did that . . . *for me*," June said in astonishment.

Oh, boy.

I shrugged. "It was nothing."

It was an answer without fully admitting to anything. Probably the closest I'd ever come to a confession to someone outside of my inner circle of thieves. The move almost made me pause. Why *was* I trusting this girl I barely knew with one of my biggest secrets? It was a risk I never would've taken back in the day of Dad. Then again, it was Dad's plans that had left me in this situation to begin with.

But for reasons I couldn't quite explain, I *wanted* to let June in a little. Not all the way. I wasn't about to say, "Hey, I'm Frankie, and I'm a former international thief turned local burglar, and I might want to be your friend. You in?"

Still, I had to admit, I had the urge to not completely lie to her face.

I groaned.

This was totally Uncle Scotty's fault. He and his do-gooderness was rubbing off on me. And I hadn't even seen it coming.

"Let's just . . . forget any of this even happened," I added, hoping this would end the conversation.

"But it *did*!" June exclaimed, eyes wide. "You helped me out, even though you could've gotten caught—"

Ollie stopped short and held up a single finger.

"No-no-no," he said, waving it in front of June's face. "Frankie *doesn't* get caught."

"Oh, geez," I said, raising my eyes to the sky to keep from yelling for him to shut up already.

But I also didn't deny it. Because he was right. I didn't get caught.

At least I hadn't, until now.

"Hey, June?" I asked, cutting in before any more of my extracurricular activities could be revealed. "Remember how you said that you wanted to pay me back in some way? Any chance that offer still stands?"

June opened and then closed her mouth again. Finally, she nodded emphatically. "Of course," she insisted. "Anything. Just name it."

"Any way I could get a copy of your new app? I won't share it with anyone or anything. I just think it could . . . come in handy? For personal reasons, I mean."

She was nodding before I'd even finished.

"Great, thanks," I said with a smile. "I can give you my phone now and then pick it up from you later?"

"No need," she said. "I have, like, a dozen burners at home. I can just load one up and give it to you tomorrow."

"Since when does everyone just have disposable phones lying around their houses?" Ollie asked, looking from June to me in bewilderment. "When did that become a thing, and why didn't I get the memo?"

I chuckled. June was the only person outside of myself that I'd ever known to stock up on untraceable communication devices like they were toilet paper in a pandemic.

Maybe we'd be friends after all.

"Awesome," I said. "Thanks, June."

"It's the least I can do, considering what *you* did." She didn't elaborate any further, but we all knew what she was talking about.

"Well . . . ," I said, looking around for a distraction. Finally, I glanced down at my watch. "Shoot. Lunch is almost up. Ollie, weren't we supposed to go by Mrs. Hazel's?"

"We were?" Ollie asked, confused.

I turned to June in explanation. "I was thinking of signing up to do costumes this year."

"Since when?" Ollie asked, the shock clear on his face.

"*Since* I realized we should do something that *you love* for once," I said, giving him a look. "Besides, I'm all about dressing for the part."

June and Ollie both took in the outfit I'd chosen that morning. Ripped skinny jeans, a black-and-white tee that read *QUAND ON N'A PAS CE QUE L'ON AIME IL FAUT AIMER CE QUE L'ON A*—a French proverb that meant: When one doesn't have the things that one loves, one must love what one has—and an oversize, button-down, wool sweater that gave off serious Mr. Rogers vibes.

When I saw the doubt on their faces, I pulled a pair of sunglasses down over my eyes and smiled.

"What?" I asked nonchalantly. "I'm channeling an international girl of mystery."

"Oh!" June said, nodding like she was trying to be supportive. "Okay. Well, I should get over to the lab myself. Mr. Rizer wanted to see me about Alia anyway."

"Cool," I said. "We'll see you later?"

We waved goodbye and started to walk away, but after a few steps I heard June clear her throat.

"Frankie?" she started tentatively.

I turned back to look at her.

"I'm not going to say anything, you know. To anyone."

I didn't answer her, but nodded my head in appreciation. It was all the understanding we needed. Then we turned and went our separate ways.

As we walked, I shivered in the cold. My butt felt numb, like it could freeze off at any second. I'd stashed my jacket in my locker before lunch, a move I was regretting now that we'd fled the building. I pulled my sweater more tightly around myself and jumped up and down a few times to get my circulation going.

"Jumping for joy?" Ollie asked, smiling broadly.

"Huh?" I asked.

"Just, it's pretty obvious you're as excited as I am to be joining the show. Now we can spend every afternoon together and then I can just come back to your place after school until your uncle kicks me out. Why didn't you tell me you were interested in doing the musical—"

"Awww, Ollie, you're so cute," I interrupted, linking my arm in his and then booping him lightly on the nose with my fingertip. "You know that was just for show. I mean, me? Getting involved in a school function? No, thank you. I just needed an excuse to exit our convo with June, so you and I could have a more—dare I say it—lawfully questionable *tête-à-tête*."

"Oh," Ollie said, pulling his arm out of mine gently. "Yeah. Of course."

"Come on, O," I said, trying to bump my hip into his but missing because he'd moved. "Theater is *your* thing. Not mine."

"Exactly," he said. "Silly me, thinking that maybe you'd finally taken an interest in *my* passion for once, when I'm always so willing to dive into yours."

"But *my* passion is fun," I said jokingly. "And you like it too. So, win-win."

"You're right," Ollie said flatly.

We walked in silence for a few beats, and it dawned on me that what had started out as a light discussion had turned into something else entirely. And I was beginning to get the feeling that it was my fault.

"I'm sorry, did I do something . . . *wrong*?" I asked, totally perplexed by the direction things had taken.

"Not at all," Ollie said, jutting his chin out.

"You're mad," I surveyed. It wasn't hard to decipher this. Ollie wore his emotions on his sleeve. He was easy to read in that way.

Harder to read in others.

Ollie sighed. "I'm not *mad*," he offered. "I'm—I don't know—maybe a little disappointed?"

I tried to blink back my surprise, but I couldn't hide my emotions either. Not from him, anyway. He was the one person in my life I didn't have to do that with. No way was I giving that up.

"Disappointed how?"

I hadn't meant for it to come out sounding so defensive, but it still had.

Ollie glanced over at me before training his eyes on the building looming in front of us.

"Never mind," he said, shaking his head.

"No," I answered, reaching out for him and forcing him to stop. "Tell me, Ollie. What did I do?"

"You didn't *do* anything, Frankie," he answered, sounding tired. "I was just . . . excited by the thought of teaming up on my turf for once."

"Oh," I said quietly. "Okay."

"Forget it," Ollie said, starting to walk again.

I didn't say anything else until I'd fallen into step beside him and matched my stride with his.

"I'm not sure if this makes up for anything, but I've decided to take your advice and do something about the whole admissions stuff," I said, breaking the silence.

This made Ollie's head jerk my way.

"Really?" he asked, sounding hopeful and maybe just a tad bit excited, too.

I nodded.

"Yeah," I said. "You really got through to me."

Ollie raised an eyebrow. "I did?"

"Oh, yeah!" I answered, enthusiastically.

When he shot me an unconvinced look, I gave in. "Fine. It was *mostly* what you said, and just the tiniest bit what Annabelle said about her always getting her way."

"Uh-huh," Ollie said knowingly. "Sounds about right."

"No, but you *were* right!" I exclaimed. "It's *not* fair. Just because the whole system needs an overhaul doesn't mean we shouldn't hold individuals accountable for their actions. Annabelle's dad and his friends deserve to pay—and not just to get their kids into school. I'm sick of entitled rich people thinking that they're more deserving because they have money. People like that need to be stopped. And I'll do it one shady person at a time if I have to."

"All right," Ollie said tentatively. He seemed interested, but I could tell he wanted to hear the whole pitch before he signed up for sidekick duty. "So, what did you have in mind?"

I let out the breath I'd been holding and smiled.

"That's the thing," I said. "I was thinking we'd come up with this plan . . . together."

Entry Twelve

I'd stuck my earbuds into my ears as soon as I'd left school. Most days I walked home instead of letting Uncle Scotty pick me up. I reveled in the time to myself and looked forward to this daily ritual where there were zero interruptions. It was when I did my best thinking.

And today I had a lot to think about.

We had a new mark. Well, marks, actually. I was nearly buzzing with excitement as I ran through all the ways I could bring the Faux Four—the nickname in my head I'd given Annabelle's dad and his friends—to justice.

It had been a minute since I'd planned a heist with so many moving parts. And while it was already proving to be a challenge, I was oddly energized. The whole thing was going to be like a puzzle.

I *loved* puzzles.

As I ambled down the street, I bobbed my head to the playlist that Ollie had made me. He'd been sending me playlists that he'd painstakingly curated ever since Christmas break, and while I'd had doubts about his taste, they were all surprisingly good.

Like, really good.

Each one had a different vibe meant for a specific mood. This week's was my favorite by far, though.

The first time I'd heard "Bohemian Rhapsody" by the band Queen I was nearly knocked off my feet. But in a beyond amazing way. The song was like being on a roller-coaster ride while listening to multiple songs all in one. It was melancholy one minute, theatrical and totally unexpected the next.

Few things surprised me anymore. Yet, the music from this band, who'd been around long before I was born, had managed to disarm me. And then when the song had finally ended—nearly six minutes after it had begun—I was left breathless and feeling like I'd just run a marathon.

Then I'd immediately listened to it again.

By now I knew all the words by heart and sang along to the rock opera like it was my own personal anthem.

I was nodding my head along with the climax of the song when I saw Uncle Scotty's house—my house now too, I suppose—appear in front of me. I slowed as I started up the walk, surprised to see Uncle Scotty sitting outside on the front porch like he was waiting for me.

Only, there was somebody else with him.

"Kayla!" I exclaimed, grinning at her as I ran toward the porch. "What are you doing here?"

As soon as I said it, I realized how it sounded, so I rushed to backtrack.

"I mean, I'm happy to see you, of course," I explained quickly. "It's just—well, *why* are you here?"

Then my heart dropped into my feet as I thought of the cat that I'd adopted over the holidays. Geronimo was a gray Maine coon who had been living at Kayla's animal rescue called The Farm. I'd met her when Ollie and I had been volunteering there over winter break. And while she liked to give Ollie a hard time, the cunning, fluffy ball of fur had taken a liking to me.

At first I'd rejected the idea of taking Geronimo home when Kayla had first suggested it. Thieves didn't set down roots. And a pet was definitely a root you had to stick around for. It wasn't so much the responsibility of taking care of an animal that had worried me. It was the knowledge that if I said yes and brought her home, that was it. We were stuck here.

And I hadn't been sure I wanted that.

But then things had changed—I had changed—and suddenly Geronimo was mine.

Well, technically she was the family cat, but I was the one who took care of her, and it was my head that she slept on at night. I couldn't even remember a time when I'd come home and she *hadn't* been there, hiding in the shadows, just waiting to pounce on me as soon as I walked in the door.

The thought of not having her around—well, I couldn't even go there.

"Did something happen to Geronimo? Or The Farm? Oh, God, it's bad, isn't it?"

I raced up the steps, taking them two at a time like the house was on fire.

"Where is she?" I asked, looking at Uncle Scotty and trying to read his face for a sign that it was bad news. But his expression was blank.

"Calm down, Frankie," Kayla said with a little laugh. Then she lifted her arms and pointed down at her lap.

There was Geronimo, my fearless, fat cat, curled up on Kayla, and pretending to sleep. I knew she was pretending, because her left eye opened just enough to see that it was me before closing it again.

She was okay.

"Oh, thank gosh!" I exploded. "Do *not* do that to me again."

"*We* were just sitting here," Uncle Scotty pointed out. "*You* were the one who thought of the worst-case scenario."

"Because Kayla's here!" I countered with a gesture. "Why would she be here if there wasn't something wrong with an animal?"

"Um, I just came by to see how this gal was doing," Kayla said, scratching Geronimo behind the ears affectionately.

The cat purred loudly and then stretched into a yawn before cuddling back into her lap.

"She's also due for her shots," Kayla added. "So, figured I'd bring them by and just do it while I was visiting."

"Oh," I said, my nerves starting to calm back down.

I made my way over to where they sat, side by side. I was less frantic now that I knew everyone was okay and gave Geronimo a little pat before hopping up onto the railing, my back to the street.

"So, what you're saying is that you missed us," I said to Kayla playfully, giving her my best innocent kid impression.

Kayla laughed out loud and the sound made me laugh, too. She had that effect on people. When you were around her, you just couldn't help but be in a good mood. She was infectious in the way a Disney musical was.

"Something like that," Kayla answered, still chuckling as she snuck a glance over at Uncle Scotty, who turned his head away like he was mortified.

"We're not making you uncomfortable, are we, Uncle Scotty?" I teased him. Then, to torture him some more, I started making funny faces at him until he started laughing too. Finally he put his head in his hands so he couldn't see me at all.

"Stop!" he yelled, but I saw the smile on his face.

"Fine," I said, hopping off my perch. "But I don't know how you ever thought that you could go to clown school with such a low tolerance for embarrassment."

As I bounded away and into the house I could hear

Kayla tease Scotty with: "You wanted to go to clown school?!" My grin grew even wider as her loud cackle followed me inside and up the stairs to my room.

Only then did it start to falter.

Because as soon as I closed the door behind me, my eyes fell on the trunk at the end of my bed. The one that held all my alternate personas. My AKAs. Every costume I'd ever donned, every wig I'd ever worn, it was all stashed in my oversize red trunk.

Bits and pieces of every job I'd ever pulled were inside this box.

I ran my hand along the outside gently, feeling the coarseness of the wood beneath my fingertips. It was cooler than I'd expected it to be, especially along the metal latches that held it all together.

I wanted to open it, but I knew there wasn't time to get lost in the past. Right now was about the future, and the plan that was already beginning to form in my mind.

I knew I'd told Ollie that we would brainstorm this plan together, but so many ideas were already swirling around inside my head that I knew I needed to get them out or risk going crazy.

I pulled out one of my burner phones and clicked on an app at the top that was labeled HOMEWORK. As soon as my finger had left the screen, a box popped up in one of the corners with a bar that was blinking. When people saw the app on any of my phones, the last thing they were thinking was that it was a secret app where I had recently began keeping my notes or ideas for jobs. I typed in my passcode and then started to write.

I was looking at four separate marks for this job—which meant breaking into four houses, stealing money or valuables from four estates, possibly turning four people in to the authorities. A small price to pay to make sure that the kids who'd worked their butts off to get into their dream schools, weren't pushed aside for those who didn't earn it.

A small price to right such a huge wrong, yes. But not a small task to pull off.

It would require four totally different plans, since each house was different. I'd already done some prelim work on Brooks's house, but I'd still have to research property layouts for the others, as well as dive into the backgrounds of each.

The longer the to-do list got, the more I began to question my decision.

I closed the app and collapsed back onto my bed.

It was useless to start on anything before I even knew who we were dealing with. And to find that out, we needed to be a part of the meeting that the Faux Four were having that night.

We were going to have to break back into Annabelle's.

Entry Thirteen

I skidded to a stop in front of where Ollie was trying hard to hide in the shadows. I hopped off my bike and adjusted the bag that was slung across my back.

"We really need to have a refresher course on the art of being covert, Ollie," I whispered loudly enough for him to hear. "I could see you from a mile away."

"Well maybe I *wasn't hiding*," he clapped back as he stepped into the light of the overhead street lamp. "If I'd been trying to disappear, you would've known it."

As soon as he said it, he realized how silly it sounded and made a face.

"I mean, you *wouldn't* know it, because I'd be hidden," he clamored to save face.

But it was too late. The damage had been done.

"Right," I said, trying hard not to smile. "Now that we've established that you *weren't* hiding back there near the bushes, can we get going?"

"Hey, I'm the one who's been waiting out here for *you* to show," he argued, holding up his phone so I could see the time.

9:30 p.m.

"How did you get here so fast?" I asked him.

I pulled my bike up onto the sidewalk and hid it in the nearby bushes. Someone would only be able to see it if they really started to dig around in there. I thought about pointing out to Ollie that *that* was how you made something disappear, but I could tell he wasn't in a jokey kind of mood.

Instead I said, "I thought we were gonna leave at the same time."

"We did," Ollie answered, matching my stride as I walked in the direction of Annabelle's house. "But I took an Uber."

I stopped walking.

"An Uber?" I asked him, disbelievingly. "You're lying."

"Why would I be lying?" Ollie asked, confused. "It's cold as ice cream out here and Annabelle's house is so far from mine—"

"Mine too, but I still didn't call a car service," I said, pinching the bridge of my nose in frustration.

"What do you have against Uber?" Ollie asked.

I started walking again.

"I don't have anything against Uber," I answered, sighing. "I *do* have a problem with leaving any evidence that we were *here* in the hands of some random driver."

"But I used a fake account to book the car," Ollie argued, confused. "I learned *that* from you."

The corner of my mouth lifted just a bit, even though I knew he couldn't see me in the dark.

"At least *some* of what I've been teaching you has

stuck," I answered, punching him lightly in the arm. "Look, it's good that you used a fake profile, Ollie. But you're not in costume, which means that the driver knows what you look like."

"Oh," Ollie said, slowly. "Crud-buckets."

I saw the look of dejection on his face and forced a smile onto mine.

"Hey, I doubt he was even paying attention to you," I offered, though I didn't really believe it. "Just wear a disguise next time. Or ride your bike."

We walked the rest of the way in silence, watching our breath come out like clouds of smoke in the cold night air. Ollie was right about one thing. It *was* freezing.

"There it is," I said when Annabelle's house finally came into view.

"Wow," Ollie said as he took it in. "Definitely fit for an evil queen."

"No joke."

I motioned for him to follow me across the street to the wall I'd scaled the night before. We crouched down beside the stone barrier and I got busy pulling things out of my bag.

"You're sure they're all going to be here again?" Ollie asked as quietly as he could.

"Yep," I said. "Heard them plan it before I left last night."

Ollie nodded. "So, how are we getting inside?" Ollie asked.

I looked up at the wall behind us.

Ollie started to laugh. When he saw that I wasn't joining in, the smile fell from his face. "You've got to be kidding, right? Please tell me you're kidding, Frankie."

"Can't exactly go in through the front gate, now, can we?" I asked him, motioning to the sole camera that was visible outside of the property.

"But me waking everyone in the neighborhood with my screams because I've fallen off a wall and broken my coccyx is a better option?" he asked, sounding slightly hysterical.

"Do you even know what a coccyx is?" I hissed, stopping to look at him.

Ollie paused. "No," he admitted finally. "But I know that it would hurt if I *broke it*."

I rolled my eyes and stood up. Ollie followed my lead reluctantly and pushed himself off the ground. Just as he was straightening his clothes, I took the sharp, pointy object in my hand and lunged at him.

"Whoa!" he screamed at me, nearly falling back down to the sidewalk.

"Shhhh!" I whispered, my finger to my lips.

Ollie patted his body with his hands as if he were trying to confirm that he was still alive. Once he was satisfied, he shot me an incredulous look. "Are you crazy?"

Instead of answering, I pointed behind him at the steel spike that was now sticking straight out from in between two stones in the wall. Then, without waiting for a response, I drove another spike up above it, and then another and another, until there was a clear path of them leading all the way up the side of the wall.

I climbed up first, showing Ollie the route that he should follow as he made his way up to join me. It was a lot like rock climbing. Only on our own terms, and if we did happen to fall, it wouldn't be to our deaths.

"Think of it as your chance to finally be a ninja," I whispered down to him as beads of sweat formed on his brow.

"I only wanted to be a ninja because of the outfits," he shot back, his breathing strained as he started to climb.

He finally got up and over the wall, landing with a thud on the other side. Before he could start complaining about his coccyx, I jumped up and began to move across the lawn silently.

I peeked inside the house using the same window as before. The one that looked directly into the lavish kitchen. When I saw the security system was off this time, I gestured for Ollie to follow behind me and took off toward the smaller door situated right next to the house alarm.

"We're just going in through the back door?" Ollie asked, barely loud enough for me to hear.

"Yep," I said, and slowly lifted my hand to the knob and turned it.

I wasn't at all surprised when it opened easily. Wealthy people often thought that if they had a wall around their property that it negated the need for common safety precautions. This was, of course, wrong. In fact when a thief saw a fence around a house, they saw it as the universe circling something important. Like a bull's-eye.

I pulled the door open a crack and put my ear to the gap. There were no sounds inside. Just silence. Giving Ollie a thumbs up, I opened the door all the way and slipped into the air-conditioned kitchen.

It felt like we were walking right into the refrigerator, itself.

I shivered as I waited for Ollie to join me where I was hiding behind one of the islands. He bumped into me clumsily as he got situated, but instead of pushing him off me, I welcomed the small bit of body heat he provided.

"Where now?" Ollie mouthed to me when I didn't move again right away.

"The Bahamas?" I mouthed back. "Where it's warm?"

Ollie wrinkled his nose and stifled a laugh.

Knowing we had to get on with it, I rushed across the kitchen and into a dark doorway in the corner. Just beyond it was a staircase that I took two at a time on quiet feet, while Ollie bounded up after me.

When I'd been planning tonight's recon, I'd realized that I hadn't yet schooled Ollie on the ins and outs of my grappling launcher, and so we'd needed a less flying-through-the-air mode of entry into the house.

This was when I'd zeroed in on the staircase just beyond the kitchen. I'd discovered it the night before when I'd been fleeing Annabelle's. It directly connected the kitchen and the second floor where all the bedrooms were. And also led to the same landing where I'd eavesdropped.

I stopped short at the top of the stairs and looked in the direction of Annabelle's room. Her lights were off. Which likely meant she was either already asleep or not home. With this knowledge, I led Ollie to the open landing area and coaxed him into laying down flat on the floor and sliding himself forward until he was next to me. He struggled a bit at first, and then ended up going with a more inchworm approach, but finally we were both settled into place.

Just in time for the show.

Once again the Faux Four had taken up residence around the table of flames, and each had a drink in hand. This time, though, there was a heaviness in the room that hadn't been there the night before. The woman named Connie was sitting so tensely in her chair, I got the feeling she was ready to flee at any moment. Dakota was gripping his glass so tightly that his fingers were white, and Lily . . . well, Lily downed one glass of a bright red liquid before promptly refilling it. And then she downed that one, too, and poured another.

"Whoa!" Ollie breathed quietly.

I didn't shush him because tonight there was music on in the room below, and any sound we made would be muffled. The song was classical and unobtrusive, which *would* make for good background noise while they were discussing all the ways to break the law.

"I know," I whispered, miming like I was guzzling a drink. "Someone's thirsty."

Ollie cocked his head to the side quizzically. Then he shook it. "No, not that. Him."

I followed Ollie's finger as he pointed down at one of the men below.

"You didn't tell me that one of the dads was *Dakota Max*!" he said excitedly.

"Because I didn't *know* that one of them was Dakota Max," I said back. Then I added, "Who's Dakota Max?"

"Really?" Ollie asked, shocked. "You don't know who he is?"

"No," I said with a little shrug. "Should I?"

"Uh, yeah!" he whispered. "What have you been doing, living under a rock?"

"No," I said flatly. "I was on the run from the cops on account of all the robberies and all."

"Right," Ollie said, shutting his mouth.

"Well?" I asked him when he didn't say anything else. "Who is Dakota Max, then?"

"Only one of the biggest movie stars in the biz," Ollie said, like I should know this.

"What's he been in?" I asked.

"I think the better question is: What *hasn't* he been in?"

"Just tell me," I said, starting to lose patience.

"Okay, okay," he said. "Dakota Max is probably one of the biggest stars Hollywood has seen in the past twenty years. He started to act in his teens, but transitioned easily into more adult roles as he got older. Mostly ones that involved big action scenes. There's this one franchise he's been doing for the better part of a decade now, and it's won all these awards."

"Ugh, I hate those kinds of movies," I said, sticking out my tongue.

"You might be the only one who feels that way," he said, showing me his cell screen, which was displaying the amount of money Dakota's last movie had made.

"Wow," I said, impressed. "With that kind of cash, he could just buy his own school."

"Isn't that sort of what he's doing?" Ollie asked.

"Fair enough," I answered. "I still don't get why so many people like those kinds of high-action flicks, though. The girls are never put in charge, when clearly they're the smarter ones. And everyone's always so unreasonably attractive. You should see some of the people I've met over the years in my kind of work. Let's just say they're *not* winning any modeling contests."

Ollie blinked.

"But we're cute," he offered. "And we're sort of like action figures."

"We're not at all like the actors in those movies," I pointed out.

"Speak for yourself," Ollie said softly with a far-off

look. "They should totally make a movie about us."

I turned to stare at him.

"They definitely should *not*," I answered.

"I would play myself, of course," Ollie continued, ignoring me.

"There's not going to be a movie about this!" I hissed more loudly than I'd intended.

We both looked down at the cast of characters below us, hoping they hadn't heard our bickering. And then I let out a small gasp.

"One of them's gone," I said, feeling my body grow even icier.

"No," Ollie said, the fear oozing from his voice.

I counted the heads again.

One, two, three . . . person number four was for-sure missing.

"He must've heard us," I said, scurrying to push myself up as quietly as I could in my current panic. "We have to go."

"But—" Ollie said, trying to stand up himself.

"Now," I said. "We have to go *now*!"

"Well, hello there," a voice boomed, suddenly closer to them now. "We've been waiting for you."

The words made me want to run, but there was nowhere for us to go.

We were trapped.

Entry Fourteen

I didn't run. I couldn't. Instead, I just stood there, frozen to my spot. Ollie finally scrambled up from the ground and hustled over to where I was still standing. He knocked into me, forcing my feet to move and my mind to snap back to the present.

"Let's go!" Ollie said, tugging on my arm.

I paused.

"Wait."

"Wait?" Ollie asked, totally confused. "You just said to run."

"Now I need you to get back down and wait," I commanded.

Ollie crouched and stopped moving. "I'm so confused."

"Come on in and take a seat," Brooks's voice rang out. Now I could tell that his words were echoing from downstairs.

I hesitated and then slowly made my way back over to the landing.

Peeking out, I could now see that another person had joined the party. He was skinny, and had a head of short gray hair and a slightly hunched back like older people often got. But when I got a look at his face, I realized he couldn't have been a day over fifty, maybe.

"Please, take a seat," Brooks said to the man and gestured to the seat that he'd vacated earlier. "Would you like a drink?"

The man waved off the chair.

"That's all right," he said. "I prefer to stand. Keeps the blood pumping."

"Your call," Brooks said, filling a short glass with amber liquid and handing it over.

The man took it gratefully and brought it to his lips. When he finished drinking, he swirled around the contents and examined it.

"Good stuff," he noted, and then gave it another taste.

"Only the best," Brooks added before going back over to his chair and sitting down.

The new man walked around the room for a few seconds, taking in each of the Faux Four one at a time. He was wearing a dark blue tracksuit and pristine white sneakers. It looked as if his hair had a hat dent in it where a hat should've been. Even without it, he looked like he'd just stepped off the sidelines of a basketball court.

"Mr. Admissions is going by the wrong nickname," Ollie said as if reading my mind.

"Right?" I agreed.

And then as if on cue, he started to give his opening speech.

"I'm sure Mr. Valera has told you why I'm here,"

he said, pacing in front of them. "Just like I know that you've reached out to me because you're interested in finding out about my unique . . . *services*."

"Which are?" Lily asked, wrapping one arm around her midsection while the other clutched to her drink like it was an additional appendage.

"Now, Lil," Brooks chastised her. "This is our guest. He's not one of your clients that you can grill and then charge two hundred and fifty dollars an hour for it."

The men in the room chuckled like they were all in on the same joke, while Lily pressed her lips together tightly and Connie fidgeted in her seat uncomfortably.

"No. I'm afraid my services are of a different price range," the man responded with a leering grin.

"And what exactly do we get for our money?" Lily asked, her voice hard. It was clear she had not appreciated being dismissed by a man—any man—and she would not be silenced. "I mean, I'm aware that you claim to be able to get anyone into anywhere, but how do you do that exactly? What's your secret?"

Her friends looked around at one another like they'd expected something like this from her and were maybe a little embarrassed by the crassness of her questioning. But Mr. Admissions held up a hand before they could say anything about it.

"That's fair," he answered, still smiling. I could see that it didn't extend to his eyes though, which meant that the gesture was only that. It wasn't genuine. "But it's also fair to say that if I told you all my secrets, then I wouldn't have the successful business that I do, now would I?"

The men laughed again and Lily just sunk back in her chair, clearly unsatisfied with the answer.

"With that said, I *will* tell you most of what I do," Mr. Admissions added when he saw that he might be losing Lily completely. "That way you know how it works and what you're paying for."

Lily stared at him a bit longer until she finally nodded. It was a small gesture, but it was enough for the man.

"So, we'll get right to it, then. People call me Mr. Admissions. They do this because I can get any kid into any school in the country," he said, beginning to walk around the room again.

"Brag much?" Ollie muttered, and I smiled.

It was obvious that this was Mr. Admissions's wheelhouse, where he felt most comfortable. Pitching to potential clients. Bragging about how good he was at what he did. Being the center of attention. This was where he excelled.

"But let me give you a little background first. Most schools—and I'm talking universities and private institutions alike—offer two modes of entrée," he said. "One: You go in through the front door. Fill out your applications and hope your kid's grades and extracurriculars are good enough to get them in. I'm guessing by the fact that I'm here though, that this is not a viable option for you."

The Faux Four didn't make eye contact with each other, unwilling to admit out loud that as rich and powerful as they were, they were unable to get what they wanted without outside help. When none of them objected, Mr. Admissions went on.

"Two: You go in through the back door. 'Donate' millions of dollars to the school for a slightly better chance of getting them to send you that letter that says, 'Congratulations! You're in!' And even then, there's no guarantee."

He said this and splayed his hands like the very thought of it was ridiculous. And it was. But so was what he was doing.

Whatever that was.

"And what? Your way goes in through a trapdoor or something?" Dakota asked, laughing at his own cleverness. When nobody joined in his laughter, he hid his awkwardness by clearing his throat deeply.

"Not through a *trapdoor*—though that *is* witty," Mr. Admissions said, winking at Dakota as he threw him a bone. The actor broke out into a smile, accepting the compliment like it was a glass of water in the desert. "No. If you go with me, I'll take you in through the *side* door."

"Isn't it hoops that you're supposed to jump through for these kinds of things?" Ollie whispered as he placed his chin on his folded arms and settled into a more comfortable position. "When did this whole business with doors start?"

I smirked.

"No clue. With the exception of tonight, I rarely use doors to break into places myself," I said. "I don't want *anyone* to see me coming or going."

"Amen to that," Ollie added.

"Through my foundation"—Mr. Admissions was talking again—"I would create a point of entry into the school of your choosing. I do this either through the existing personal relationships I have at the institution in question, or through my exclusive abilities to persuade people to see things my way."

"In other words, blackmail," Lily chimed in, her words just a little slurred. She looked almost bored by his presentation. Like none of what he was saying seemed to surprise her—or impress her for that matter. "Or perhaps, you just straight out threaten them?"

Mr. Admissions looked at her coolly like he was growing annoyed by her attitude. But whatever he was thinking, he didn't say it out loud.

"Now, I've gotta leave a little something to the imagination, don't I?" he said instead. I caught the eye roll from Lily as she lifted her glass for another drink.

"As far as *how* we get students in, there are certainly more avenues available to us at the college level, including walking onto a sports team or by having a trusted outside party take the client's standardized tests for them to ensure an agreed-upon score," he said, but waved both of these points off as quickly as he brought them up. "In the case of private schools, I tend to use my connections, along with a sizable 'donation' from my foundation to guarantee admission. Of course, the 'donation' originates from you."

“Forgive me, but that sounds a lot like going in the back door,” Brooks said with a frown. It was the first time since he’d welcomed him inside that he seemed to be questioning Mr. Admissions’s abilities. “What do you do that we can’t just do ourselves?”

Mr. Admissions grinned to show that the question didn’t bother him in the slightest.

“Now that’s a fair question—a *smart* question,” Mr. Admissions said, pointing at Annabelle’s dad like he was the one to watch. “You’re going through me because, frankly, I have connections you don’t. I know exactly who to offer your donation to in order to get you what you want. But by all means, if you’d like to give it a go yourself, feel free.”

Brooks looked around at his friends’ faces and it was like they were all silently communicating. Finally, he turned back to Mr. Admissions and nodded.

“We’re in,” he said.

“Excellent,” Mr. Admissions said, rubbing his hands together briefly before clapping excitedly. “Here’s what I’ll need from you—”

A sudden rush of noise cut him off midsentence. I couldn’t immediately decipher what was happening, but then all five heads pivoted in the same direction as if on cue. Ollie and I found ourselves leaning forward to try to see what they were looking at, but it was a pointless endeavor.

Without getting up from his chair, Brooks called out, “Annie, honey, come on in here and say hello to everyone.”

“Annie?” I mouthed to Ollie while raising an eyebrow.

For a second, I wondered why she insisted on going by Annabelle at school, instead of the more youthful nickname her dad had just used. But then I gave up wondering. The girl was weird. Who knew why she did the things she did?

"Hi, Daddy!" Annabelle's voice rang out sweetly.

"Annie, sweetheart, you know everyone," Brooks said, motioning to his friends.

Annabelle had placed her hands into the hidden pockets of her dress, but took one of them out to give them a wave. They all smiled at her. Well, everyone but Lily, who was struggling to reach out and grab the bottle in front of her.

"Here, let me help," Annabelle said, quickly rushing into view and then grabbing the glass container carefully. With the ease of a practiced veteran, she went over and filled the woman's cup without spilling a drop.

"Cheers, Annie," Lily said, holding her glass up to her. Then, as if she remembered that Annabelle's hands were empty, Lily took a drink for both of them. "God, if only my boys were more like you. So pretty and obedient. You're lucky, Brooks."

"Mm-hmm," Brooks murmured noncommittally to the comment before waving Annabelle over to him. "Come, Annie. I want you to meet Mr.—"

He stopped short as he realized he wasn't sure what to call Mr. Admissions to those who didn't know what he did for a living.

"Call me Bill," Mr. Admissions said, holding out his

hand to shake hers. She did and then stepped back out of sight.

"Nice to meet you," she said politely. "Do you work with my dad?"

It was an innocent enough question, with a much more complicated answer. But it seemed like Mr. Admissions was used to covering up his identity from those not in the know, and he didn't hesitate before answering.

"Something like that," Mr. Admissions said, smiling at her. "Your dad has told me a lot about you."

She beamed at this. "He has?" she asked, the hope in her voice so obvious that it bordered on embarrassing.

"Of course!" he insisted, his eyes falling squarely on her. "He was just saying how *smart* you are. And *driven*."

I almost snorted out loud at this, which would've gotten us caught for sure. I managed to swallow it down in time.

Annabelle's own face slowly twisted until it looked like someone else's. "Are you sure he wasn't bragging about my stepsister, Clara? She's sort of the pride and joy of the family."

"Nope," Mr. Admissions said, moving toward her and playfully tapping her on the nose. "It was all you. Swear to God."

Annabelle frowned.

I wasn't sure if it was because she could tell he was lying or because he'd just touched her without asking. She didn't move for a few seconds and I wondered if she was going to go off on him.

But then her face erupted into an enormous grin.

"Thanks, Daddy!" Annabelle said innocently, and bounced over to give him a hug. The man hesitated briefly before putting his arms around his daughter awkwardly and patting her roughly on the back. If she noticed his discomfort, she didn't let it show.

Brooks shot an embarrassing look at the adults in the room before clearing his throat loudly and adjusting his position in the enormous chair.

"You girls staying the night?" he asked once Annabelle finally put some distance between the two of them.

Girls?

"No, sir," a squeaky voice let out.

That's when I saw that two other figures had snuck forward at some point during Annabelle's awkward exchange with her father.

Because of *course* Annabelle wouldn't go anywhere without her minions. She never did. From what Ollie had told me, Gladace and Penny had been by Annabelle's side ever since the first day of kindergarten. Literally. Gladace always on the left and Penny always on the right. How any of them could even stand one another for one day, let alone seven years was a mystery to me. After seeing Brooks's penchant for throwing money at problems, I wouldn't have put it past him to have Annabelle's only two friends on the payroll.

It would explain a lot, actually.

Then again, Gladace and Penny weren't exactly

attractive friend candidates, so maybe that was it. Every queen needed her loyal—and silent—followers.

"Ugh," I said under my breath.

"Double ugh," Ollie amended.

"I so got lucky in the sidekick department," I said, knocking into him affectionately.

I'd meant it as a sweet compliment, something to express how much I appreciated him and his friendship. But as soon as I saw his face I knew it had been the wrong thing to say.

"Sidekick?" he asked, frowning. "Is that all you see me as? Someone to do your bidding, like them?"

"That's not what I meant, Ollie," I said, training my eyes back on the group below. We couldn't afford to miss anything here. Not when so much was at stake.

"Really?" Ollie continued, his voice cold. "Because that's *exactly* how it sounded to me."

Down below us, I could see the three blurry figures fidgeting.

"Why don't you girls head upstairs to Annie's room until your parents get here," Brooks suggested, though it was clear they weren't being given a choice in the matter.

"Sure, Dad," Annabelle said, trying to hide the hurt in her voice.

"Ollie, you need to go," I said, pulling out my camera and starting to take pictures of everyone in the great room.

"*What?*" he whispered in disbelief. "Just because

I don't want to be a mindless zombie who follows you around—"

"Don't be silly, Ollie," I said, standing up as I shoved my phone back into my pocket.

"Bye, Mr. Valera!" Gladace called out.

Or maybe it had been Penny. I honestly couldn't tell the difference.

"So now you're calling me *silly*?" Ollie asked while I was trying to document everything.

"Ollie, you need to go," I said, looking through the pictures on my camera.

He looked at me like I'd told him he looked fat in his outfit. But I didn't have time to worry about his hurt feelings.

I grabbed both his arms and shook him. "Annabelle and the other two are on their way up here and they are literally going to step on us if we *don't get moving*."

Ollie's mouth, which had been hanging open just a moment ago, slammed shut and he began to race as quietly as he could toward the back staircase. I was practically on his heels within seconds and prayed to my namesake, Frank Abagnale Jr., that he didn't trip and go tumbling down the stairs.

Then we'd *really* have something to worry about.

Somehow we made it down the stairs without falling and zipped across the kitchen so fast, I swear we would've looked like a flash of light if a camera had been on us.

We didn't say anything as we ran to the wall and

scrambled up and over, taking care not to fall funny as we jumped to the sidewalk below. And then we took off again, unwilling to slow down until we were out of sight of the house.

When I was sure we were out of danger of being caught, I slowed to a walk. My chest burned from our escape, so I placed my hands on top of my head to make it easier to breathe. When it began to help, I stopped where I stood and willed my heart to slow.

Surprisingly, Ollie continued to walk, barely slowing down to catch his breath. I knew he had to be hurting. I was ready to collapse, and I trained for this stuff.

"Ollie," I called out after him.

He acted like he couldn't hear me.

"Ollie!" I yelled, hoping it would startle him enough to make him stop.

It didn't.

I let out a growl and took off after him again. When I caught up, I grabbed his arm and spun him around hard.

"What is your problem?" I asked him, annoyed that he was pulling this during a job.

Ollie seemed surprised to see me standing there. "Man, you're freakishly strong," he said through gasps of his own.

"I work out," I said with a little smile.

Ollie began to grin back, but then remembered he was upset and abruptly frowned.

"Ollie," I started, but he held up a hand to cut me off.

"No, Frankie," he said. "What you said back there? It wasn't cool."

"What did I say?" I said, feigning confusion.

"You said I was your *sidekick*. Not friend. Not partner. Sidekick."

Oh.

"Poor choice of words, I admit," I said after a moment, trying to smooth things over. "But you know I didn't mean it the way you're taking it."

Ollie crossed his arms over his chest and narrowed his eyes.

"So, it's *my* fault you don't think before you speak?" he spat.

I flinched.

"Whoa, Ollie, come on," I said, starting to get defensive myself. "I said I was sorry. Why are you making this into such a big deal?"

He took a step backward while still facing me.

"Because I'm sick of being treated like I'm less than you," he said, his lower lip trembling a little. When he saw me glance at his mouth, he turned his back on me so I couldn't see whatever happened next.

And then I felt awful.

I went to reach out to him again, but he was already too far away from me.

"And by the way, you never actually said you were sorry!" he shouted at me before stomping off without looking back.

Entry Fifteen

I was still trying to figure out what the heck had just happened when I hopped off my bike thirty-five minutes later. I couldn't feel my hands or face, but underneath my jacket, I was sweating. Probably from a mixture of adrenaline and the long ride I'd had to make just to get back to Uncle Scotty's.

Either way, all I wanted to do was climb in through my bedroom window and disappear under my covers—gross sweat and all.

I didn't even bother to look up as I walked my bike slowly down my quiet street. Usually I would've loved the solitude on a night like this; walking along in the silence with nothing but my thoughts to keep me company. Only, right now, my head was mostly filled with regret.

Why had I said that to Ollie?

If only I'd chosen a different word than *sidekick*. Then again, I hadn't thought that I would ever have to censor myself around him. We were close enough now that I could say things to him that I couldn't say to anyone else. Before tonight I would've sworn he'd always know what was in my heart. Who I really was.

That despite my poor choice of words, he'd know I'd never say anything to deliberately hurt him.

Right?

He *had* to know I thought of him as my equal and not someone who was there to do whatever I told him to.

I mean, he *did* do whatever I told him to most of the time, but that was because we were always pulling a job or preparing to pull a job. And the reality was, I knew more about the thieving world than he did. Somebody had to take the lead in these things, and given my background, it made the most sense that it would be me.

Then again, why was I supposed to grovel over what had just been an innocent mistake? It wasn't like I'd told him he was worthless or had bad style. I'd called him a *sidekick* for crying out loud. How was *that* worth fighting with me over?

And hadn't *he* been the one to call himself the very same thing on multiple occasions? In the beginning he'd wanted to be my sidekick. Begged to be, even. So why was he suddenly so mad over the term?

And was he really so mad about what I'd said that he was willing to jeopardize our entire friendship—and our current case—just because he was feeling a little less important? If he was, then I guess our friendship hadn't been as strong as I thought.

And, well, who's fault was that then? All mine? I don't think so. It takes two to make a friendship. I shouldn't have to tiptoe around him just because he has issues he obviously needs to work through.

Suddenly a new thought came to me.

Maybe it wasn't about tonight at all. Maybe Ollie's display of temporary insanity was *actually* about the other day and him not getting the lead in the musical. Now that made more sense to me than him getting angry over an innocent comment.

The more I considered all this, the more it dawned on me that none of what had happened earlier was about me. It was all about Ollie. As usual. Maybe it was me who should be annoyed.

I finally looked up as I felt the anger begin to rise in my chest over the whole Ollie thing, but when I did, I promptly rushed over to the shadows of the sidewalk.

I hadn't noticed it before because I'd been so thoroughly entrenched in my rage-spiral, but now I could see that our house wasn't completely dark like I'd expected it to be.

The lights were still on downstairs and the porch glowed warmly, making it easy to see that there were two figures outside the house, sitting on the bench.

What the—it couldn't be.

Was it?

It *was*.

There, sitting together under the cover of night was Uncle Scotty and . . . Kayla.

"She stayed?" I whispered to myself confused.

Earlier that night, after giving Geronimo all her shots, Uncle Scotty had invited Kayla to stick around for take-out. I'd expected her to refuse, but she hadn't. This in itself was a little weird, since she usually stayed late at The Farm to take care of the live-ins and newcomers.

And I'd sort of been under the impression she had no social life outside of work, since she'd never talked about friends or doing anything that a normal woman her age should be doing.

So, when she'd said yes to our invite, I'd been pleasantly surprised.

As we'd sat down to Chinese takeout I'd briefly wondered if we were about to have the most awkward dinner of all time. Uncle Scotty wasn't exactly big on the talking side of things, unless he was interrogating. Our first month of living together had been excruciatingly uncomfortable until we'd found our groove.

But tonight Kayla had made things easy. She was friendly and relaxed and seemed happy to keep up more than her side of the conversation. This suited us introverts perfectly, but even we seemed to come out of our shells once it was clear there was no pressure on us to do so.

The conversation between Uncle Scotty and Kayla had been effortless too, which was kinda shocking. At one point, my uncle was laughing at something Kayla had said about scooping up poop, and I'd wondered whether I'd walked into *The Twilight Zone*.

But this was what Kayla did. She was one of those people that everyone liked. There was no controversy there, no traits that would annoy or alienate a person. She simply fit in wherever she went.

I just hadn't expected her to fit in so well at our house.

And now I was discovering that she hadn't gone home after I'd said good night and gone to my room. And then snuck out.

I ditched my mode of transportation in our neighbor's yard, knowing that between all the stuff their five kids left strewn around the property, they wouldn't notice yet another bike lying on its side.

Then I crept closer, crouching low as I ducked behind the shrubs that divided our yard from our neighbors'. Moving alongside it as silently as I could, I finally stopped once I was close enough to see what was happening.

And hear it.

"And then of course, she denied that she had anything to do with it, but come on, this is *Frankie* we're talking about," my uncle said. "If anyone was going to be able to pull something like that off, it would be my niece. She has a talent for these kinds of things."

I leaned farther into the bush, realizing they were talking about me. I squinted through a patch of the leaves and branches until I could see them, sitting side by side.

They looked comfortable.

Like it wasn't their first time.

But that was impossible. They'd barely known each other before Ollie and I had volunteered that winter, and I'd hardly seen Kayla myself over the months since. Besides, it wasn't like Uncle Scotty ever had anyone over. . . .

Did he?

If I hadn't snuck back home so late, I never would've known that Kayla had stayed to hang.

Was it possible that Uncle Scotty had a whole slew of friends I didn't know about? Did he throw dinner parties and movie nights once I'd fallen asleep?

"Frankie?" Kayla said, my name echoing through the night. I froze. "You think your niece has a talent for setting off water sprinklers without leaving a trace of evidence, just so she could set a scene for her friend's performance? Seems like you're giving her a lot of credit here."

"You don't know her like I do," Uncle Scotty said quietly.

"You're right," Kayla agreed, shrugging. "I only spent *every day* with her over the holidays, watching her take care of abandoned and injured animals. Though there *was* this one time when she was tossing treats to the dogs in the yard and I thought to myself, 'Now *this* girl clearly has some evil genius in her.' "

Her voice was dripping with so much good-natured sarcasm that I couldn't help but smile. She was ribbing Uncle Scotty the way that I did. And I liked it.

He needed someone to balance out his serious side.

I was glad they were becoming friends.

"Okay, okay," Uncle Scotty said, throwing his arms up in surrender. "I get what you're saying. I just—well, she didn't have the most conventional upbringing and I worry that I'm not enough to help her overcome her past."

Kayla nodded.

"Or maybe she just needs someone to love her exactly how she is," she said softly.

He smiled at her before turning his face straight again and staring at the quiet street. They sat there a moment in silence, the only sound around them, the rhythmic creaking of the swing they were on. Finally, Uncle Scotty spoke again.

"You know I'm never going to say you're right," he said seriously. Kayla glanced over at him as he broke out into a goofy grin, and then she smacked him in the arm hard. "Ow! I thought vets were supposed to be nice!"

She narrowed her eyes at him.

"We are," she said. "To *animals*! But humans? We don't care about you."

Uncle Scotty broke into the kind of laughter that I'd only heard on rare occasions, when it was clear he was having fun or enjoying himself. The fact that Kayla had orchestrated this one herself, impressed me.

I pulled back from the bushes and continued down the length of the shrub, making sure to step lightly and avoid any obvious debris that might alert Uncle Scotty and Kayla to my presence. Sure, I didn't want to get caught having snuck out of the house, but I also didn't want to interrupt . . . whatever I'd stumbled upon.

Once I got to the gap in the property, I slipped through and walked over to the sugar maple that sat majestically next to our house. It was a gorgeous tree, big and full, with these fat branches that seemed to span the length of our yard.

Not long after I'd moved in, I'd suggested we fasten a swing to one of the sturdier branches. Uncle Scotty had thought it was a great idea and it had kicked off one of my favorite uncle/niece bonding times so far. After sitting in some stain that we'd used to paint the board, and then falling on our butts after not tying a tight enough knot, the Lorde house finally had a useable tree swing.

Uncle Scotty still didn't know that I'd only suggested the swing so I'd have a mode of escape from my room after hours.

I stepped up onto the wooden seat and gripped one of the ropes as high as I could and then jumped. It had only taken a little bit of practice to build up the muscles and stamina needed to shuffle my way up to the top. By now I was a pro and could do it in ten seconds flat.

I was totally going to kill it when we had to do the rope climb in gym class.

Once I reached the tree limb, I gripped the bark tightly and then eased my legs up and over the branch. I stood up slowly, making sure that I had my balance before I started to walk.

I'd done this so many times that I probably could've done it with my eyes closed. But I didn't. There was no need to show off when there was nobody around to impress.

When I was close enough to the house, I extended

one of my legs out in front of me, reaching it toward the windowsill. Once my foot made contact, I leaned forward like I was stretching my calf muscle, and pushed the window up carefully. The first time I'd ever opened it, the squeaking sound had been terrible. I'd immediately greased it and had kept it up every week since. There was no point in going through all the trouble of scaling a tree if you were just going to wake everyone when you opened the window.

I pulled myself inside and then cautiously lowered my body to the floor of my bedroom. It was dark in here, too, save for a lamp on the side table that I could control with an app. It had a sunrise feature that I preferred to Uncle Scotty's way of waking me up.

He liked to blast the song "Friday" by Rebecca Black right outside my door. On repeat. Until I surrendered and came out of my room. And if you haven't ever had to wake up this way, count yourself lucky. It is *not* pleasant.

I'd just collapsed on top of my bed after having shed my drenched and smelly clothes when my phone buzzed.

I picked it up without even thinking about it, assuming it was Ollie wanting to tell me about some celebrity who'd broken up with another, or a new movie that we had to see. But as I was bringing it up to my face, I remembered our fight earlier and frowned.

Maybe he was texting to apologize.

But when I read the screen, I realized it wasn't Ollie at all.

Hey, Frankie! It's me, June.

I finished downloading the app onto the burner phone for you.

I was wondering if you have time to come by my place before school tomorrow to grab it.

I have something I think you'll be interested in seeing and I can just hand off the phone then.

I blinked at the screen as I scrolled through the messages.

I was pretty sure I'd never given her my phone number, though she could've easily asked Ollie for it. Not sure why she didn't just ask me for it, but whatever.

It was weird, but not so weird that I was going to write her off as a creeper.

So, I programmed her number into my phone and then wrote her back, my thumbs flying across the keyboard of my phone like they were in a race.

Shoot me your address and I'm there.

My eyes were already starting to drift closed as I finished the sentence and hit send. Then I passed out.

Entry Sixteen

"Who's this June girl again? Have I met her?" Uncle Scotty probed nonchalantly as we waited at a stoplight the next morning.

When I'd requested a ride to a friend's house—one other than Ollie—he hadn't asked me any questions. Just nodded and asked me when I needed the ride. At the time, I'd known the interrogation would come, but I appreciated the brief respite from having to spill everything that was going on.

We'd been in the car less than five minutes before he'd broken the silence.

"Remember that girl whose invention was stolen before the contest for that private school?" I answered, trying to make it sound like there was no more to the story than that. "That's June."

But of course, Uncle Scotty wanted more.

"Oh, yeah," he said, acting like he didn't recall every single detail of when I'd first mentioned it. "How'd that end? Did she get it back?"

I knew what he was doing, but there was no way of getting around playing his game.

"Yep," I answered, not giving any details. That was

the number one rule when talking to a cop—or any adult in a position of authority, actually. You never gave more information than you had to. Answer the questions they ask, but nothing more. Anything else and you might as well just put the handcuffs on yourself.

"Did she win?" he asked, looking over at me.

"She did," I answered. Then, so he didn't start to wonder what I was keeping from him, I threw him a few inconsequential details. "June's really smart. Probably the smartest person our age. She created this app that combines social media with facial recognition technology. It's pretty dope."

Uncle Scotty raised his eyebrows, surprised. "Someone your age is creating apps? With facial recognition? We don't even have access to that at the station."

He muttered the last part, sounding just a tad bit jealous.

"A police station that's behind on technology?" I said, my voice sounding shocked. "No way!"

Uncle Scotty rolled his eyes.

"Tech will never replace good, old-fashioned detective work, Frankie," he said, but I could tell it was forced.

"Uh-huh," I responded, the corner of my mouth lifting up. "If you say so."

"I do," he said, a glint of mischief in his eyes. "So, Ollie didn't come over this morning for breakfast."

"Nope," I said, turning my head away so he couldn't see my reaction.

He was as good at reading facial expressions as I was,

and I wasn't ready for him to know what was going on yet. Not when I was still confused about it, myself.

"Everything okay?" he asked.

"Yep," I said, before turning back to face him. This time it was with a grin on my face. "So, having Kayla over last night was fun. Seemed a little weird that she showed up, though. Out of the blue like that."

Uncle Scotty's eyes bounced over to me.

"She wanted to see you and Geronimo," he said. "What's so weird about that?"

I shrugged. "I don't know. Maybe the fact that she's never just stopped by before? I didn't even know she knew where we lived," I said. "Did you?"

He paused a second before answering. This was a total Uncle Scotty thing to do. He was gathering his thoughts, trying to choose every word that came next, carefully.

Interesting.

"I think I gave it to her after you volunteered there," he said. "In case we wanted to ship stuff to the house for Geronimo."

"Makes sense," I said out loud. But in my head I was thinking it was a convenient response.

I was about to ask him a question that I was dying to get the answer to when the car pulled over and stopped in front of a baby-blue-colored house. It was about the size of my own, but more cookie-cutter. A glance up the block told me that all the houses were made from the same developer, since the only thing that kept them from looking identical was the paint jobs for each.

"Here we are," Uncle Scotty announced, putting his car in park.

"Thanks," I said, pushing open the door and getting out.

"June's folks are driving you to school?" Uncle Scotty called out through his window as I walked around to the sidewalk.

I nodded, though I wasn't *entirely* sure how we were getting to school. It was a detail that didn't matter much to me. Not when there was the mystery of what June wanted to show me hanging in the air.

As I strode up her walkway, I waved my hand in the air to signal to Uncle Scotty that he could leave. But he didn't. Behind me there wasn't any crunching of tires against rock and asphalt, no happy honking of a car horn. Instead, there was just the hum of an engine sitting idle.

I rolled my eyes as I knocked on the front door and waited for someone to answer.

I heard some banging around inside and then a thump and a scream.

The hairs on my arms stood up and I felt myself go rigid with concern. Should I charge in? Go get Scotty?

Before I could decide on anything, somebody was opening the door in front of me.

It was a boy about the age of five and he was the spitting image of the Campbell's soup kid. Curls sprang from all parts of his head like the springs of a Jack in the box.

"I'm Phillip Bentley Langer. Who are you?" he said in his young, squeaky voice.

"Oh!" I said, smiling down at him. "Well, nice to meet you Phillip Bentley Langer. I'm Frankie Lorde."

"Are you God's assistant?" he asked, tilting his head to the side curiously.

I let out a surprised laugh. It was the most creative question I'd ever been asked about my name and I liked the boy instantly.

"No," I answered, easily.

"But you're a Lord," he argued.

"I am." I nodded in agreement.

Then I crouched down so we were eye to eye and looked around carefully to make sure nobody could hear us. Phillip Bentley Langer leaned forward, somehow sensing that I was about to tell him a secret.

"I'm a Lorde of thieves," I whispered.

The boy's eyes grew wide and his mouth dropped into an O. It was the exact reaction I'd been going for.

"Like . . . Robin Hood?" he breathed, equally as quiet as I'd been before.

I paused and scrunched up my face as I thought about this.

"Actually, that's exactly what I'm like," I agreed.

Now it was his turn to pause.

"But you're a girl," he said.

"I am."

"And Robin Hood's a boy," he continued.

"He is."

"Then how can you be like Robin Hood?" he asked.

"I'm not," I said.

"But you said—"

"I'm not *like* him," I repeated. "I'm *better* than him."

Phillip Bentley Langer closed his gaping mouth abruptly like I'd just dropped a bombshell on him.

"Whoa," he let out, like I was a mythical creature not unlike a unicorn or Spider-Man.

"Philly?" a voice called out from inside the house. A second later, June appeared at the door. "Philly! You know you're not supposed to answer the door by yourself. What if Frankie had been a *bad person*."

"She's not," he argued, looking up at her defiantly. "She's Robin Hood."

June shook her head and raised her eyes to the ceiling. "She's not Robin Hood, Philly. This is my friend Frankie. She goes to my school."

Phillip looked between me and his sister, but didn't argue.

"Now go find Mom. She needs to get you dressed for school," June said, mussing up his mop of curls before smacking him on his behind lightly.

The boy began to do as he'd been told, but just before he could duck out of sight, he looked back at me curiously.

I brought my finger up to my mouth and mimed a *shhhhh*.

His mouth formed a cheeky smile before he disappeared from view completely.

I turned to look back at Uncle Scotty, who was still waiting in his car at the curb. I pointed at June and then gave him a thumbs-up to show him that he could leave. He held up his hand in a goodbye and then pulled away.

Following June inside, we headed down a hallway and to a closed door off to the side. She opened it up and gestured to the stairs that led farther down into the house.

"Cute kid," I said as I took the wooden steps carefully.

"Philly? Yeah, my mom always says, 'It's a good thing he's cute,'" she said, a smirk in her voice. "'Because otherwise she'd give him back.' She's joking, of course. But he's the biggest imp, my brother."

I nodded in agreement.

As my feet hit the basement floor, I slowed until I nearly stopped, incredulous at what I was seeing.

In front of me was what could only be described as a lab. And not just some test tubes on a table, though there were certainly those, too. We were talking electronics, multiple computers, random tools and metal parts, and a whole slew of items that were unfamiliar to me.

A crazy image of June as a mad scientist popped into my head and I chuckled before I could stop myself.

"What?" June asked as she glanced over her shoulder at me.

"Nothing," I promised, before starting to roam the room. "So, *this* is where you do your thing?"

"I guess you could say that," she answered, sitting down at a desk in the middle of the room and fiddling with something I couldn't see. "It's my inventor's space. I modeled it after Thomas Edison's lab, but then added some modern elements."

I wandered around in wonder, taking in all the odds and ends stashed around the room. My knowledge of technology was limited to the gadgets I used on my jobs, so I had no clue what half of the stuff was that I was seeing.

"It's . . . impressive, June," I said finally, drawn to a flat box on a nearby counter.

It looked a little like a hot plate—one of those kitchen appliances that heated up food when you didn't have a stove or microwave—but that's where the similarities ended. Because directly above it, hovering in midair, was another, smaller platform, circular in shape. Four spotlights were trained on an object being suspended a few feet above the table. As I got closer, I realized what it was.

"My siblings are always stealing my snacks," she explained as she saw me staring, wide-eyed, at the pile of chocolate candy bars on top of the floating silver disc.

I reached forward and ran my hand through the empty space underneath it. Nothing happened except that the display began to turn in a slow circle, until we had a 360-degree view of her stash of Snickers, Hershey's, Twix, and Reese's bars.

"Cool, right?" she asked, suddenly right beside me now.

I jumped in surprise as she pressed something flat and cold into my hand. Looking down, I could see that it was a cell phone. The burner she'd programmed for me.

"The app's on it," she said, already walking away.

"Thanks," I said, glancing at it before shoving it into my back pocket. "Your lab is really cool, June. And I'm honored you've inviting me into your . . . inner lair. But you could've just brought the phone to school."

June smiled widely.

"But then I wouldn't have been able to show you this," she said, motioning for me to join her on the other side of the room.

I followed, my curiosity piqued.

There, side by side on a copper bench, were three separate items. I got the feeling that they were each placed strategically in some kind of order, like a display case at a jewelry store.

"Ta-da!" June yelled, throwing her arms out wide like a magician at the end of a trick.

I stared.

"Sorry—what am I looking at?" I asked, shaking my head.

"These are for you," she said with a flourish.

My head whipped around to her, sure I'd heard wrong.

"Okay," I said slowly. Then, feeling a little stupid that I had to ask, I added, "Um, what are they?"

"Right," June said, slapping her palm to her head like she was a dunce. Then she moved over to the first object, which was a pair of boots. They were big and chunky and had a bunch of straps to secure them closed. Sort of like biker boots, but not quite. I looked down at my own Chucks and then back up at the boots June held in her hand.

"I appreciate it, June," I said, trying to find the right words. "But they're not really my style."

June started to laugh.

"They're not for fashion, Frankie!" she cackled, snorting loudly. "They're for function."

"Meaning?"

"Meaning," June repeated, "that these are like that rotating shelf over there. They're *levitation* boots."

"What!" I exclaimed, unable to hide my shock. "Like, I can just put these on and . . . *fly*?"

"Well, not exactly fly," she explained. "But you will be able to suspend in the air a bit."

"So cool," I breathed as I took the shoes from her and looked them over.

"I know, right?" June said happily. Then she moved on to the next object on display. "And this is a modern multipurpose tool."

I looked at the thing lying in the palm of her hand.

"It's lip gloss," I said flatly.

"Yeah," she said, nodding. "But it's also a camera, a lockpick, and a stun gun."

I gasped.

"I know!" June cut in before I could say anything. "But there's more."

She tossed me the lip gloss, which I almost didn't want to catch since one of its features was a stun gun, and picked up the last item on the coppery surface.

It was a tiny little piece of metal, about the size of a dime, with a short prong sticking out of it. "You know those voice changers? The ones like walkie-talkies that change the sound of your voice like in that horror movie? Well, this is like that, except you plug it into your phone, and it can change your voice into anyone else's on the planet."

"Are you kidding?" I asked her. "How?"

"You just record the person's voice onto your phone and this little gal will turn your voice into theirs," she finished, standing back and placing both her hands on her hips like a superhero.

I looked at her in awe for several seconds. I couldn't think of what to say that would adequately express what I was feeling.

Finally, I spat out, "Would it be super weird if I told you I kind of love you right now? Like in a completely fangirl kinda way?"

June plopped down onto her copper bench, looking relieved by my reaction.

"Not weird at all," she said with a goofy grin.

I looked at all the cool gadgets in my hands, and then something dawned on me.

"June," I said slowly. "Not that I don't love all this, because I definitely do, but . . . why did you think I'd want this stuff? I mean, sure, it's all really cool, but it seems sort of meant for a specific kind of person. What made you think that person was me?"

It was the most roundabout way of asking her if she knew who I really was. I mean, I would've been lying if I hadn't wondered about a hundred million times since learning about her Who'sThat app, whether she'd used it on me and found out about my . . . complicated past. I'd been dying to find a way to ask her without arousing suspicion, and this might be my best chance at bringing it up without sounding any alarms.

June shrugged and looked down at the ground like she'd been caught doing something bad.

"I don't know," she answered softly. But then she suddenly looked up again and her eyes locked on mine like she could read my mind. "I guess I just had a feeling that this kind of stuff might come in handy. You know, for . . . *whatever*."

I nodded as this sunk in.

"You know June, they just might," I agreed, hugging all my new treasures tightly.

Entry Seventeen

I ran into Ollie before school. We seemed almost shy as we walked toward each other, like two people who shared a secret that they both wanted to forget.

I told myself that it was silly to be nervous to talk to him. This was Ollie. *My* Ollie. The same guy who barely registered the mean things that kids said about him around school. The kid who'd still wanted to be my friend after finding out who I was and what I did with my spare time.

So why was my stomach in knots?

I hadn't had time to think about what I'd say to Ollie when I saw him again, since I'd been so engrossed in my visit to June's. And then she and I had chatted on our way to Western, making it impossible for my mind to wander.

But as soon as I saw him walking toward me just outside the entrance, a hundred different thoughts rushed through my head in seconds. Should I still be upset that he'd gotten so mad over nothing? What about the things he'd said about me? Was he sorry? Was he still mad at me? What if he ignored me? Should I just apologize and hope we could both move on?

And the worst question of all: Was our friendship over?

As we stopped in front of each other, I wished that I could read his mind. And then I remembered that I could.

Well, not read his mind. But I could read his body language.

Instead of letting my eyes drift toward the ground sheepishly, I forced myself to look at my friend instead. Before he'd dropped his own focus down to the pristinely white loafers he was wearing, I'd caught him blinking more than usual. Both of these things—rapid blinking and eye contact avoidance—were classic signs of guilt.

I know I should've felt bad about this, but all it did was fill me with relief.

He regretted what had happened as much as I did.

"Hey," I said softly.

"Hey," he replied, equally quiet.

We were both silent for a few seconds. I decided to be the bigger person and go first. If I was being honest, it was a lot easier to apologize when you knew the other person felt bad, too.

"Look, O," I said, tentatively. "I'm really sorry about what happened last night. I never would've said what I did if I'd known you were going to take it the wrong way."

Ollie's eyes drifted up to me.

"I'm not sure I actually took it the wrong way," Ollie said cautiously. I could tell that he was being careful with his words, too. "But I *do* know that you didn't set out to hurt me or my feelings."

I shook my head emphatically.

"I didn't. I swear," I said. Then, just to prove it, I held out my smallest finger to him. "Pinky promise."

"You're such a weirdo," Ollie said, rolling his eyes before entangling his finger with mine. "You're lucky I like weird."

"I am," I said to him, hooking my arm with his and then resting my head on his shoulder. "Lucky, I mean. To have a friend like you."

I wasn't usually this mushy, but after the drama from the night before, I felt like Ollie needed it for us to get back on track.

"I know," Ollie said seriously. "I'm pretty amazing."

We both started to laugh.

"Get a room!" a voice rang out, cutting through our beautiful moment.

We both turned to see Annabelle standing there, hand on her hip, minions beside her. They all wore identical looks of annoyance, something they weren't trying to hide at all.

"Annabelle," I said, not at all surprised that it was her spitting the venom. "I know you wish you had a beefcake like *this* on your arm, but there's no need for you to be *ugly* about it."

Annabelle gave us a disgusted look.

"First off, ew," she said, sticking her tongue out like she was gagging. "Second, beefcake? Please. More like *beefy*."

She and her toadies burst out laughing, and I began to pull my arm away from Ollie's so I could go after her. Enough was enough. She needed to be taught a lesson.

But Ollie beat me to it.

"Annie," Ollie said sweetly. "I hope your dad wasn't *too* disappointed in you when you told him that you lost the Alia competition. I mean, it's not your fault that your sister is practically a genius and that you're just, well . . . you."

The three girls abruptly stopped laughing. Ollie's slam hit its target better than he could've hoped. When Annabelle finally spoke, it was between clenched teeth and with embarrassment in her eyes.

"She's my *step*sister, you *Stranger Things* rejects," she hissed, walking slowly and deliberately toward us. "And don't you talk about my dad. *Ever*."

"Looks like someone has daddy issues!" I singsonged, just to twist the knife in a little farther.

"At least I *have* a daddy," Annabelle shot back, eyes blazing. "You can't say the same, can you, Frankie?"

A playful shriek from another student cut through the air at that exact moment, distracting me long enough so that by the time I'd turned back to Annabelle, she was already walking away. I wanted to race after her, push her down in front of everyone. Humiliate her. Tell her she was wrong. Make her stop being so nasty. Make her pay for everything mean she'd ever done.

But none of that would actually solve anything.

And it might just end up getting me into trouble, which would result in Uncle Scotty jumping all over my case, and I *definitely* didn't want that. The last thing I needed was a detective watching me closer than he already did.

So, I walked away.

"She's such a little. . . ," I started to say, so angry that I couldn't think of a single insult that quite fit her.

"Toad-licker? Ninnyhammer? Mumblefutt? A gray sprinkle on a rainbow cupcake?" Ollie supplied for me.

I burst out laughing.

"Mumblefutt?" I exclaimed. "What does that even mean?"

He paused before answering.

"No clue," he admitted. "But it sounds like it fits her, doesn't it?"

"You know, oddly, it does!" I agreed, nodding.

Ollie steered me up the school steps and in through the front door.

"You have anything before classes start?" I asked him as we weaved through the throng of students who were all here early. "I have some stuff to fill you in on."

"Oooooh, intriguing," Ollie said, rubbing his hands together devilishly. "I was going to study for the math quiz today—didn't exactly get much done last night as you recall—but I could skip it. Math isn't my thing anyway."

"My dad always told me that all you need to know is how to count your money," I said, pulling him into the library and through a labyrinth of bookshelves.

"Your dad is a smart guy," Ollie said, smiling.

When we arrived at a small table in the corner, away from prying eyes, I climbed up onto its top and faced the room, my feet resting on a chair. Ollie didn't wait for an invitation. He did the same.

"So, June gave me her new app this morning," I told him, pulling out the burner and touching the screen so it lit up. I purposely didn't tell him that I'd gone to June's house to get it. Without him. I didn't want him to think that I'd been auditioning for other friends. Not when we'd just made up.

"Sweet," Ollie said, leaning his head in toward mine so he could see what I saw. "So, what've we got?"

"It's an app that can take a picture of anyone and tell you who they are using facial recognition and—"

Ollie cut me off.

"You don't have to go all techy on me," he said. "Just tell me why we want it."

"We want it because besides Annabelle's dad and that movie star guy, we don't know who Mr. Valera's other two friends are," I explained. "And if we don't know who everyone is, we can't take them down."

"Gotcha," Ollie said nodding. "And this app?"

He gestured to the phone in my hand.

"It can tell us just about everything we want to know about each of them," I finished.

"Go June," Ollie said sounding impressed.

"Right?" I answered. "You know, I think she might

be someone we can trust. Maybe not with all our secrets, but definitely with some of them."

Ollie looked at me, a shocked look on his face.

"Since when do you trust anyone but me?" he asked.

"I don't," I promised. "I was just saying . . . June might be an ally. I mean, she's totally aware that we broke into Annabelle's and she hasn't said anything to anyone yet."

"Well, maybe that's because we did her a solid by getting her project back," Ollie suggested. "You don't bite the hand that feeds you."

"I think it's more than that," I said. But then I shook my head. This wasn't the time. "Anyway, what do you say we find out who the ladies of the Faux Four are."

"Let's do it!" Ollie nearly shouted and pumped his fist in the air.

Shushes echoed between the stacks of books and we both made faces before getting to work uploading the pictures I'd taken the night before.

What came up was more than I'd expected, and not what I expected, all at the same time.

It was like a having a Wikipedia page for every person ever, regardless of their celebrity status. Only, it was so much more than that. It covered the basics of course: name, childhood, relationship status, claims to fame. But then it also listed the obscure stuff: online searches, arrests or run-ins with the law, photos both authorized and unauthorized. Anything that had ever found its way onto the Internet or social media was there at the click of a button.

I, for one, would've been toast if it ever landed in the wrong hands. With that said, the downright amazingness of June's app for someone like me? Priceless.

We went down the list one by one, starting with Brooks, and couldn't seem to read fast enough.

BROOKS VALERA

Age: 46

Occupation: Hedge fund manager at Simon & Roe

Personal Life: Married to Lizzie Thomas (1993–2001)
Married to Tina Vasquez (2007–2015)
Married to Arabella Fogue (2015–present)

Children: Annabelle Valera (with Tina Vasquez), age 12, attends Western MS in Greenwich, CT

Clara Fogue (stepdaughter with Arabella Fogue), age 19, attends Stanford University

Net Worth: 24 million

Scandal: Brooks became Instagram official with his third wife just days after filing for divorce from his second, leading people to believe there was some overlap with the two relationships. He retained custody of biological daughter, Annabelle, when the girl's mother gave up her rights willingly. Reasons for this are unknown.

Favorite Food: Brazilian

Signature Look: Expensive suits

Click for more

LILY WADE

Age: 44

Occupation: World-renowned family therapist; *NYT* bestselling author of the book *The Perfect Family*

Personal Life: Married to Samuel Wade (1996–present)

Children: Cassius Wade, age 17, received GED after being kicked out of multiple schools

Benjamin Wade, age 11, attends Western MS in Greenwich, CT

Net Worth: 17 million

Scandal: A post on Perez Hilton revealed screenshots of Lily's oldest son, Cassius, complaining about his family on his private Twitter account. In one particularly scathing post, he called his famous family therapist mom a "bigger fraud than Donald Trump's toupee." Instagram photos show Cassius sporting a half-shaven head and multiple piercings. His social media accounts have since been deleted.

Favorite Wine: Pinot Noir

Favorite Book: Gone Girl

Click for more

CONNIE JAMES

Age: 44

Occupation: Celebrity plastic surgeon

Personal Life: Married to Derek James (2010–present)

Children: Samantha "Sammy" James, age 12, attends Western MS in Greenwich, CT

Net Worth: 21.5 million

Scandal: One super celebrity slapped James with a multimillion dollar lawsuit after he claimed his wife's new face was "too beautiful" and that it eventually led to her leaving him for someone more attractive. The suit was eventually dismissed.

Favorite App: Super Slots

Celebrity Crush: Patrick Dempsey

Click for more

DAKOTA MAX

Age: 52

Occupation: Actor

Personal Life: Married to Silvia Peetz (1989–1993)
Married to Rose Concord (1995–2000)
Married to Shelly Tudor (2007–2007)
Married to Emmanuelle Hero (2008–2015)
Currently single

Children: London Max, age 12, attends Western MS in Greenwich, CT

Net Worth: 240 million

Scandal: Two of his marriages ended because of infidelity; the *Daily Mail* has published several exposés implying that at least one of Max's marriages was arranged by his manager and was "just for show." Max's last two movies were box office flops. Has custody of son, London, whom he adopted with Emmanuelle Hero.

Number of movies starred in: 60

First car: Burgundy Toyota Corolla

Click for more

When we were finished reading up on the Faux Four, Ollie and I sat in shock for several minutes.

"That was like my favorite gossip site times a billion," Ollie said. "On steroids."

"My head is mush," I said, rubbing my eyes, which were dry from staring at my phone's screen for so long.

"So, what now?" Ollie asked.

I took a deep breath. "Now we do some recon I-R-L," I said.

"Well, at least that won't be so hard since all their kids go here," Ollie offered. "And I feel like we already know more about Annabelle than we ever wanted to."

"No kidding," I said.

"I actually know Sammy pretty well. She's a theater nerd like me. London—well, I was sort of obsessed with him because of his celeb kid status, but then I found out he was a jock. Suddenly, he doesn't quite hold the same appeal. Not that I would turn down an invitation to a party at his house if it meant getting some facetime with his dad. I mean, wouldn't it be cool if that's how I got discovered—"

"Focus, Ollie," I said, snapping my fingers in front of his face to bring him back to reality.

"Right," Ollie said, shaking the daydream away. "What were we talking about again?"

"The others?" I asked. "Who's Benji?"

Ollie shrugged. "No clue."

My mouth fell open.

"But I thought you knew everybody?" I asked in mock shock.

"I know!" he exclaimed, either not catching my sarcasm or ignoring it completely. "I thought I did too."

I chuckled a little before growing serious again.

"So how are we going to get to know these kids, get them to open up to us?" I asked.

We both thought about this in silence until all of a sudden, Ollie's face lit up.

"I got it!" he said excitedly. "There are only two current events classes for our grade. And Sammy and London aren't in my class, so they *have* to be in yours."

"Really?" I asked, scrunching up my face like I was trying to place them in my mind. But it was no use. I wasn't exactly social outside of my little bubble of Ollie.

And now maybe June.

"I'm not even sure what the Benji kid looks like," Ollie said, lifting his arms up as if the kid was a mystery. "We'll both have to do some recon there, I think."

"Well, okay," I said finally. I nodded my head as a plan began to form. "I guess I'm making some new friends."

Entry Eighteen

"Congratulations, John Derry! You've won an all-expense paid trip to Bali!" I said into the phone, my intonation coming out male and deep, thanks to June's voice-changing device.

"Seriously? I can't—is this for real? I don't even remember entering anything," the man on the other end sputtered. There was a pause and then he said the next part to himself. "Did I? I mean, I *do* like contests. . . ."

"One of your students sent in an essay telling us how you impacted their life and why you deserved a vacation," I explained, rolling my eyes. "You're a very impressive teacher. Our favorite entry by far. And now we'd like to offer you a trip to Bali."

"Wow, okay," he said, clearly surprised by the news.

And it made sense.

Mr. Derry was a good teacher—he made every lecture interesting and always chose fascinating topics that somehow actually felt relevant to people our age—but it wasn't like he was the most popular teacher at Western. That honor went to our literature teacher, Mr. Misaki.

But for my purposes, Mr. Derry was the most important teacher on campus. Because he taught our current events class. The one that some of my latest marks attended.

Only, hopefully not for long.

"This is so exciting!" Mr. Derry said on the other line. "I guess I'll have somewhere to go this year during spring break."

"In order to claim your prize, you must pack your bags now and get to the airport within four hours," I insisted.

"Four hours?" he asked, his voice nearly cracking with surprise. "But I can't possibly. I have classes to teach. How am I supposed to just drop everything and leave?"

I knew that he was really asking himself the question and didn't actually expect me to tell him what to do. So, I waited for him to work it out on his own.

After a minute of going back and forth between accepting and turning down the prize, Mr. Derry finally agreed that he would call in for an emergency leave from school and take the trip.

Ten minutes after we hung up, I'd e-mailed him his itinerary and wished him a good time. I'd paid for the tickets and resort accommodations with some of the money left over from the past two heists. Most of the money from our jobs had gone back to those who deserved and needed it most. But I had kept a portion for myself, for times like this. Sort of like a "Future Heists Fund."

Besides, Mr. Derry could use a vacation. Teaching was a thankless—and underpaid—job, after all.

Then, with one last plan still to put in place, I left

for school, a hop in my step like I often had at the start of a job.

I loved this part.

The beginning when everything was new and nothing had gone wrong yet. Because it usually did at some point.

But sometimes that was fun too.

I got to school before most of the teachers had even started to arrive. Unsurprisingly, Ollie had declined my invitation to meet me at the butt-crack of dawn, claiming he needed his beauty sleep after having stayed up late the night before to practice a song for the musical.

This was fine, though. The next thing I needed to do didn't require two people.

I slipped inside Mr. Derry's lecture hall and made my way over to his desk at the front of the room. A teacher's desk had always been an interesting thing to me. Looking at what one held inside its drawers was sort of like sneaking into a teacher's bedroom and peeking at the things in their bedside table or bathroom cabinet. It felt private, like getting to see a hidden part of them. The part they didn't *choose* to share with their students, but was there, nonetheless.

Mr. Derry's desk was no exception.

I sat down in his chair carefully, placing my hands palm down on the table top. Three piles of papers sat neatly stacked in the center of the surface. One was our homework from the week before, each with grades strewn across the top. Another was administrative stuff—

attendance, grades for past tests, flyers from a variety of school events. I ran my finger down the list of students on the class roster, and stopped when I reached the name Benjamin Wade.

Benji? Score!

The last paper I looked at appeared to be our latest assignment.

One he hadn't given to us yet.

And he never would.

I took the stack and shoved it into the oversized backpack I'd plopped down onto the floor next to me. Then I retrieved my own stack of assignments and placed it where the other had been. My assignment would put the next part of my plan into action.

I was about to get up and leave, when my interest got the better of me and I pulled open Mr. Derry's top drawer.

Inside were an assortment of basic teacher's tools: pens, pencils, a few different-colored Sharpies, scissors, paper clips, Post-its. Then there were the items that had clearly been confiscated from students. Gum, a bouncy ball, handcuffs that were clearly from a cop Halloween costume, an ancient flip-top cell phone, and a hat that said HONK IF YOU'RE HARRY.

I picked up the toy handcuffs, and then shrugging, stuck them in my bag too.

Shutting the drawer with a clang, I got up to leave.

Two hours later, just as I'd hoped, Principal Hollycooke appeared at the door to the lecture hall with an unfamiliar face ambling behind her. She was a pretty woman, definitely on the younger side. Possibly fresh off a university campus where she'd earned her degree.

Both women marched down the side of the room, only stopping when they arrived at the podium just off to the side of Mr. Derry's desk. The sub looked nervous and excited, like a student on her first day of school. Principal Hollycooke looked . . . well, she looked pissed. Like having a teacher call out for a few weeks had been the last thing she'd wanted to deal with that day.

Sorry, Hollycooke. It had to be done.

Almost all the students were already seated, some weary of what they were seeing at the front of the room, others fascinated by it.

I sat there trying to hide a grin.

Principal Hollycooke waited for the bell to ring and then promptly cleared her throat.

"Hello, students," she said, forcing a smile as her eyes roamed over us. "I'm afraid Mr. Derry will be out the next few weeks while he deals with a . . . *family emergency*."

I snickered into my hand because the emergency was that he couldn't possibly say no to a free trip.

"Taking his place will be Ms. Tridell," Principal Hollycooke said, motioning to the young woman beside her without fanfare. "She comes to us highly recommended by several schools in the area. I trust that you will all treat her with the same respect and courtesy that you would any other teacher here at Western. I also feel it prudent to mention that Ms. Tridell has the authority to give out detentions as she sees fit. So make good decisions, people."

No substitute was going to dole out detention slips, unless she wanted to be eaten alive.

Nope, Ms. Tridell would be putting up with whatever we threw at her if she ever wanted to be asked back. Which worked out fine for me.

When nobody responded, Principal Hollycooke turned and unceremoniously said, "They're all yours."

And then she rushed out of the room.

Ms. Tridell waited for the door to close behind her before she started to speak.

When she did, it was with a smile and just a slight tremor in her voice.

"Hey, guys!" she said, trying to sound upbeat.

We stared blankly at her.

"Okay then. Like Principal Hollycooke said, I'll be hanging out with you all for the next few weeks while . . . ," she said, pausing to look down at a piece of paper she held in her hand. It was obviously a cheat sheet of some kind. "Mr. Derry takes care of some personal stuff."

And I handle some business.

"Anyone want to tell me what y'all are currently working on?" she asked, looking around the room at us.

When the class remained silent, I finally raised my hand to help her out.

"I think we were going to start a new project?" I said, trying to seem unsure of myself.

"Right!" Ms. Tridell beamed at me like I was her ally.

I wasn't.

She rushed over to Mr. Derry's desk and glanced at the three piles in front of her. It didn't take her long to notice the stack I'd placed there.

She scooped up the papers and walked back over to the podium, still looking through them. Finally she tapped them on top of the desk and smiled at us.

"So it looks like your teacher has already chosen a topic of discussion and divided you up into groups of four. Your topic is: 'What is the biggest scandal of this century?'" Then she started to laugh. "Looks like all my time spent on gossip sites would pay off for this one!"

Nobody else laughed. We just stared, either embarrassed for her or bored of the whole thing completely.

"Nothing? Tough crowd," she muttered to herself before brightening again. "Okay, I'll call out each group one at a time, and you should all feel free to move around to meet your new partners. When I'm finished separating you, you can all get started. Here goes."

Ms. Tridell began to call out names in the groups that I'd created for the project. A few teams in, I heard my own name called, along with three others specially chosen for the assignment.

"Group F will be London Max, Frankie Lorde,

Sammy James, and Benji Wade," she said. As we began to stand up, she moved on to the next set of names.

I walked over to where London and Sammy were already standing and then waited an extra thirty seconds for Benji to catch up. He seemed reluctant to join, like organized groups weren't his thing.

Welcome to the club, Benji.

"All right, humans!" Connie's daughter, Sammy, barked out in what I assumed was her best impression of an evil dictator. "The topic is, 'What is the biggest scandal of this century?' Well, that's easy . . . It's gotta be Principal Hollycooke's obvious crush on lunch lady Beatrice. Am I right?"

A smirk spread across London's face and I couldn't help but sport one, too. Sammy was funny. Theatrical and over the top. But funny. She reminded me of someone, but I couldn't think who.

"All right, class," Ms. Tridell called out from her place at the front, squinting down at the paper I'd left for her earlier. "It looks like Mr. Derry was going to have you all prepare a presentation of your chosen scandal at the end of next week. He suggests you meet together outside of school to accomplish this. Visual aids are encouraged. Remember to list your sources."

I turned back to the others.

"I'd offer up my house, but it's under construction," I lied, setting things in motion.

“We can do my house today after school if you guys want,” Sammy offered with a shrug.

“I’m down,” London said, reclining in his chair. “Your mom still buy those little rolled up corn chips that look like lollipop sticks?”

Sammy raised her eyes knowingly and nodded with a smile. “The chili and lime ones? Mom’s obsessed. There’s a whole stash in our pantry.”

“Sweet,” Landon said, licking his lips.

“Cool,” I said. “So, we’ll all meet there around, say, four? Let’s exchange numbers.”

We took turns typing in our digits and then waited for Sammy to send us her address. Just as we finished up, the bell rang and we said our goodbyes.

I shoved my stuff inside my backpack, taking care not to let any of Mr. Derry’s real assignments fall out of their hiding place, and then rushed out the door and into the sea of students in the hallway.

I headed straight for Ollie’s locker, noticing that somebody else had already beat me there. I took in the faded overalls and scarf secured around the person’s hairline and then bounded toward the two mischievously.

“Hey!” I shouted as I jumped in between Ollie and June, clapping them both on the shoulders and making them jump.

“Cheez-Its!” June cried out, slamming back into the row of lockers as she scrambled to flee. When she saw that it was only me, she put a hand to her chest and let out a relieved breath.

"Hey, guys," I said with a smile.

Ollie scowled at me. He didn't like being scared, something I was reminded of every time Geronimo jumped out at him. It didn't stop me from doing it every chance I got though.

He turned back to his open locker. "What's got you so—dare I say it—*happy*?"

"Things are just . . . coming together," I said with a grin.

"Well, stop it," Ollie said. "You're weird happy."

"I like it," June chimed in.

"You would," Ollie said. He was straight-faced, but we all knew he was teasing.

"He's right, though," I said with a sigh. "Happy me is rarely seen in public."

"Like Bigfoot," Ollie added.

I pushed him lightly.

"So, what's up—" I started to say when a hush suddenly fell around us. There was such a sudden drop in noise that we all turned to see what was going on.

At first, I didn't see anything. But then the sea of kids began to part, making way for a group of men walking determinedly toward the exit.

I blinked.

Not just men.

Police officers.

And being led along behind them was another man, hands bound behind his back in handcuffs. His head was down, so I almost didn't recognize who he was. But then, just as they were passing us by, the man looked our way, giving us a clear view of his face.

"Omigosh," June breathed in shock.

"What's happening?" Ollie asked, confused by the perp parade.

"This can't be a coincidence," I say to June quietly.

She shook her head in agreement.

We all stood there, mouths open, as the janitor from the Alia competition—the one the judges used to test out June's app—was escorted out of the school by the Greenwich police.

Entry Nineteen

The arrest of Western's janitor was all anyone could talk about the rest of the day. Teachers tried to keep students on point, but it was a *point*less endeavor.

It was the most scandalous thing to happen at the school since it had opened decades before. It was certainly the most interesting thing I'd witnessed since coming here.

The police presence hadn't bothered me as much as it would have in the past. That's not to say I didn't have a mini freak-out when the blue uniforms first appeared in the hallway of my school, though. But then I saw that they had a different suspect in mind and I felt unnerved for other reasons.

The main one being that June and I both knew that it wasn't just happenstance that the same man who'd been the subject of June's Alia entry was now in police custody.

What had shown up in his profile that was so bad the police needed to get involved?

I remembered how the Alia judge had gotten a major case of distraction after choosing his victim. That he'd rushed off to show some "colleagues." Could those colleagues have been the cops?

June and I were both at a loss as to what had shown up on that burner phone, but we knew without a doubt that it had been bad.

For the second time in days, I thought about how June's app could be dangerous in the wrong hands. Of course I could also see the tremendous value in being able to meet new people, gather basic background info on strangers, and even the social aspect of how it could bring people together.

Still if the app ended up out there with the masses, I might be the next one paraded around in handcuffs. And I couldn't seem to stop ruminating on this fact, even as we made our way over to Sammy's house for our first homework session with my new project-mates.

It didn't help that Sammy had brought it up again, joking that we should present the arrest as the most scandalous thing to have happened in the past decade. I pointed out that there were bigger fish to fry and that none of us knew *why* the guy had been taken in. All this would make getting the project done by the following week practically impossible.

"Good point," London said. "Let's choose something easy."

"That's not what I'm saying exactly," I reasoned, but secretly I was with him on this. My focus here wasn't on the class project. It was on a project of my own.

For the first twenty minutes at Sammy's house, we settled in, having been led into a large den-like room.

There was a big-screen TV in the corner, and a huge couch so deep that you could lay down and sleep on it. Plush chairs were placed around the room so guests were never without a place to sit. There was a fireplace in one of the walls that sparked to life with a touch of a button. A pool table, a full-size arcade-style game console, and what I guessed was a reading nook rounded out the list of awesome touches given to the room.

"We can set up in here," Sammy had said, tossing her bag in the corner and plopping down in one of the comfiest looking chairs I'd ever seen. Luckily there were more of them and I was able to snag my own, snuggling into it like it was a cloud. All I wanted to do after that was grab a book, a mocha, and a blanket, and bask in the glow of the roaring fire.

Instead, I kept on task, forcing myself to perch on the edge of the chair as I kickstarted the group session. I wanted to hurry through some of the school stuff to get to the plan stuff.

"Okay, let's list some scandals we might want to consider for the project," I said, taking out a pad of paper and poising my pen over it.

London was sitting on top of the pool table, legs dangling freely as he happily ate handfuls of the chips he'd been so interested in before. Sammy stood behind a flowery privacy partition that was in the corner. Every couple of minutes she'd come back out with a new outfit on and ask our opinion. And Benji . . . well, Benji was sitting on the couch looking uncomfortable, like he wished he were anywhere else, doing anything else.

I stopped to survey Benji. When I'd looked at him through the lens of Who'sThat? he hadn't seemed to bring up any red flags. He was never mentioned in a negative way in the press about his mom and brother. He had nearly perfect grades and appeared to lay low most of the time. He was like a walking question mark. One that I intended to figure out. So why did his mom need help getting him into a school?

"There are the obvious ones," I said, motioning grandly with my hands. "As a result of the sexual harassment cases stemming from Hollywood, the #MeToo movement tackled women's rights, gender equality, and harassment in the workplace."

"I'm just glad I never had to deal with anyone like that creep," Sammy said, appearing from behind the shade wearing what could only be described as a sailor's outfit. "Did your dad ever do anything with him, London?"

I hadn't been sure how to broach the subject of celebrity and what it was that each of their parents did, so I was grateful when Sammy did it for me. This way they wouldn't realize I was nosing around their lives, looking for dirt.

"Dakota did a few films with him, but says he never witnessed anything himself," London answered, shoving a few more chips into his mouth.

"You call your dad by his first name?" I asked, curiously.

"I'm adopted," London said, as if this were explanation enough. "Anyways, he only likes me to call him Dad when we're in public. Makes him look less . . . rough around the edges. More of a family guy."

"Oh," I said as if I understood.

Of course, I didn't. Even though my dad always treated me like his equal, he never would've let me get away with calling him Tommy. Same went for Uncle Scotty.

"To be honest, I'm surprised Dakota never got caught up in the whole #MeToo thing himself," London said absently.

We all stopped what we were doing when he said this, surprised he'd been so candid. And what he'd implied.

Finally, London burst out laughing.

"I mean, I was surprised he didn't get *behind* the movement, of course," he said, giving us all a look that was meant to show he'd been kidding before. But the slight twitch in his cheek told me otherwise. "I didn't mean . . . well, you know."

We all nodded, trying to let him know that *we'd* gotten the joke, too. But it was clear by the uncomfortable silence that we all knew what London had really meant. It's just that nobody was willing to go there. Not right now, at least.

I covertly wrote down DAKOTA & #METOO? on one of the rear pages of my notebook, before flipping back to my project page.

"How about Trump?" Sammy asked, breaking the

silence. "And all the many, many, many, *many* ways he's acted—before, during, and after his presidency."

"Too obvious, no?" London said, back to munching on his snack.

"And too much work," I added, writing down the former president's name but putting an *X* beside it. "There isn't enough time in the world to recall all the ways he's messed up."

"True that," Sammy echoed.

"What if we went a little closer to home?" Benji asked, surprising all of us when he spoke. His voice was soft but strong. I got the feeling that he only spoke when he felt he had something to say. And with a seemingly out-of-control older brother and a mom who talks to people all day about their feelings, I could see why he kept his mouth shut as much as possible. So my interest was certainly piqued when he took this moment to speak up.

"As in?" I asked, trying to get him to elaborate.

"As in the stuff that's happened around here, lately?" he added, looking straight into my eyes. "Christian Miles for one. Or how about the Tiger Twins just a few months back? Seems like they're obvious choices to me. It's almost like there's some kind of caped crusader taking down all the bad guys in the community."

Everyone seemed to quietly digest the idea, but I was watching the spark that had appeared in Benji's eye. Like the thought of an actual hero in our town was exciting.

"I like it," I said, nodding even though I didn't actually

want anyone looking too closely at either of those cases. "But I'm wondering if we should stick to something more global? The assignment said the biggest scandal of this century. I highly doubt these small-town criminals count, right?"

Sammy sighed dramatically.

"She's right," she said. "We've gotta think *bigger*."

"And maybe keep it *away* from home?" London said, looking down into his bag lost in thought.

It was clear he didn't want anyone looking too closely into his. Maybe he had more to hide than just a privileged existence and a dad who was willing to break the law to get him into school.

I was curious if the others were feeling as much pressure to hide their family skeletons as London was.

"All right," I said like I'd had enough. "Those chips can't *possibly* be as good as you're making them out to be."

I crossed the space toward London in just a few strides and snatched a rolled-up chip from the bag before he knew what was happening. I popped it into my mouth quickly, and was instantly assaulted with a flavor explosion. The mixture of heat and sweet was a winning combo that delighted my taste buds.

I closed my eyes enjoying every moment of it.

"Good?" London asked. I could tell without looking at him that he was smiling.

"Oh. My. God!" I exclaimed. "How did I not know these existed before today?"

I leaned forward to take another, but London yanked them out of my reach.

"Wait, you're seriously not going to share?" I asked, surprised but amused at the same time. It was hard to actually be annoyed at London because the guy was so darn likeable.

"You tasted them," he argued. "So, *you* should understand why I'm keeping the rest to myself."

"You're evil!" I said, but it was with a smile on my face.

Sammy walked by London and smacked him in the arm. Then she turned to me.

"There are more in the pantry upstairs if you want," she offered. "Take a right at the door, then the second left. It's just off the kitchen."

"Thanks," I said, starting to walk away.

"You should try them with plain Greek yogurt," Sammy suggested behind me. "There's some in the smaller fridge. If you think they're good plain, they're even better with sauce."

"Noted," I said, then made a face at London. "Hoarder."

"Don't be jealous," he returned, shoving a whole fistful into his mouth.

I rolled my eyes before leaving the room.

As soon as I was out the den door, I rushed up the

stairs and made my way down the hallway. I wasn't looking for the kitchen, though. I was on the hunt for Connie's office.

I'd gleaned a lot from June's app—more than I ever could've gotten through good, old-fashioned recon—but I needed more. Like, there was the whole deer in headlights vibe she'd given off both nights at the Valeras that had been super weird. What had that been about? And why did she need the services of someone like Mr. Admissions in the first place? She was a celebrity plastic surgeon and her net worth was in the crazy millions, which would certainly be appealing to any school her daughter was applying for. And when I'd talked to Ollie about Sammy, he'd reluctantly admitted that she was just as talented as he was. She'd even landed the second lead in the *Mean Girls* musical.

So why did Sammy's mom feel like she needed to cheat the system? It didn't make sense. At least from what I could see on the surface.

I needed to dig deeper. And that's what today was about. Well, that and what was in Sammy's house that would be worth stealing when the time came to make the Faux Four pay.

The first door I came to turned out to be a bathroom. The second was the kitchen that I was actually supposed to be looking for. I skipped that one. The third was a guest bedroom or maybe a maid's quarters? The fourth was a theater, complete with plush, reclining chairs and a popcorn stand in the corner.

I was running out of doors on this side of the house when I finally found what I'd been looking for.

"Bingo," I said, looking over my shoulder before slipping inside.

The office was beautiful. Natural light spilled in from the tall, arching windows behind a mahogany desk. The two high-backed chairs in front of it were an elegant blue-and-cream design, and when I ran my hand along the fabric, it felt buttery soft. The walls were a mixture of bookshelves and what appeared to be high-end art. The overall effect was like an oasis from the stress of the outside world.

If I lived here, I swear I'd never leave this room.

I snuck behind the desk and sat down, pulling the laptop toward me eagerly. Pressing a few random buttons, I waited for the screen to come to life, simultaneously hoping she hadn't locked it.

An ugly little box popped up saying INPUT PASSWORD.

Frak.

I glanced up at the closed door, knowing it wouldn't be long before somebody came looking for me.

I cracked my knuckles and got to work.

I typed in *Sammy*.

Nothing.

I tried Sammy's birthdate: *October 8, 2009*.

Nothing.

I typed Connie's birthdate. Her husband's birthdate.

Big fat nothings.

I ran through the normal passcodes people used.

Animals, streets, nicknames—I even tried the words *face-lift* as a nod to Connie's job, but nothing worked.

Finally, I thought of one of the passwords my dad used and gave it a shot.

ILoveYouSammy

Suddenly I was looking at a photo of the James family. They were each dressed in blue jeans and white tops, looking every bit the all-American family. But looks could be deceiving.

And often were.

"What are you hiding, Connie?" I whispered to myself as I moved around her desktop freely now.

I found a folder named "In Case of Emergency" and clicked on it. Inside was a document with all their account information just in case something happened to Mr. and Mrs. James and Sammy needed to access anything. It was a really thoughtful thing to do for their daughter—and really helpful for anyone wanting to rob them.

Lucky for them, I wasn't at the stealing stage just yet.

I logged into their joint account. There was a little over ten grand in there, not a ton when you considered how much Connie was worth.

Maybe all her money was kept in her medical practice account? Business owners sometimes put the majority of their earnings right back into their companies. That could easily be the reason she had so little in the other one.

I logged into the account listed under Connie James, MD.

"No way," I said in shock.

There was only five thousand in this account.

There were no other bank accounts listed.

My phone buzzed then and I pulled it out of my pocket. It was from Sammy.

You get lost?

Sorry. I found your moms office and thought I'd check out why she's being all shady. Turns out you're flat broke. Want anything besides chips?

I quickly deleted this and instead wrote:

Sorry. Needed to find a bathroom. Back in two shakes.

It would buy me a few more minutes, but not much longer. I held my phone in front of the laptop and took a screenshot of Connie's accounts. Then I closed out of everything and stood up to leave.

I opened the door to Connie's office and began to hurry out when I ran smack into someone standing just outside.

Entry Twenty

"Ooof!" I let out, the noise escaping me before I could stop it.

"There ya go," a voice said, gripping my arms to steady me as I fought to keep myself upright. When I'd regained my balance, I straightened my clothes and stood up taller, finally looking up at the person who'd caught me.

It was Connie.

And she was smiling.

Not a devious smile or anything like that. It was actually genuine. She didn't seem angry or suspicious that a stranger was skulking around her house. In fact, she didn't seem surprised to see me at all. Curious maybe, but that was the most I was getting from her.

"Hi!" she said to me, pleasantly.

Gone was the fidgeting and nervousness I'd witnessed the nights she'd been at Annabelle's. Right now she looked bright and clear and calm. I never would've thought that *this* Connie had anything to hide.

"Hi!" I said back, trying my best to match her cheerfulness. I had no idea whether I was hitting the mark or not though, since my normal mode was typically one of jaded annoyance. "Um, I'm friends with Sammy? Well, classmates anyway. I mean, we're friend-ly. Not really friends just yet, but we *could* be? Maybe. Anyway, we have this school project with a few kids in our class and Sammy offered for us to work on it here, but then I needed to go to the bathroom. And of course, I got lost—"

"Hey, Mom!" Sammy's voice called out, interrupting my rambling. Connie and I watched as she walked up to us.

"Hi, sweetsie," Connie said, and enveloped her daughter in a tight hug. It was the kind where both parties rested their heads together like they were really feeling it. And Sammy didn't pull away in embarrassment or anything. She just squeezed her mom back for a few seconds, before letting go.

Wow. Okay. So *they* got along.

"I was just meeting your friend, uh . . . ," Connie said, and paused when she realized she didn't know my name.

"Frankie," I offered, holding my hand out to her.

She took it and pumped it gently.

"Nice to meet you," Connie said warmly.

"Frankie is in my current events class," Sammy offered, looking at me. "We have a sub this week and she gave us this assignment that we have to work on in groups."

"Gotcha," Connie said, nodding. "Good topic?"

Sammy suddenly struck a pose.

"It's *scandalous*, dahling," she said grandly, clutching at her neck like she was wearing fake pearls.

"Ooooh, well isn't that just *wonderful*," Connie answered, matching her daughter's accent perfectly.

They were cute together. Like they actually enjoyed each other's company.

Like Dad and I had.

Suddenly, I felt sad that he wasn't here too. And also a little guilty because it had been a while since I'd visited him. I'd just been so busy lately, dealing with life and running cons, there hadn't been time to make the trip.

I looked at my phone for something to distract me from what I was about to do, which was cry. I sniffed back my melancholy and then pointed to my phone.

"Well, would you look at that . . . I gotta go," I said to them. "I have dinner plans with my uncle."

"Oh!" Sammy said, sounding surprised. "Well, I think we decided on the #MeToo movement for our project. You cool with that?"

I nodded.

"Sounds like a plan," I answered, now that my own plan was fully in motion, I'd go with just about anything they decided on. "Sorry I have to leave so early. You know how cops can be. You're late for dinner and suddenly the whole force is out searching for you."

"Riiiight," Sammy said, nodding. "I remember somebody telling me your uncle's a cop."

"A detective, actually," I said, sneaking a glance at Connie to see how she was reacting to this news.

But she wasn't. Her face remained unchanged.

So, either her money problems weren't due to anything illegal or she had given herself way too much Botox and it kept her from having normal facial expressions. I had no idea which it was.

"Okay, girls," Connie said after a few seconds. "I gotta get working. Frankie, it was really great to meet you. Sammy, sweetie, I'm going to do some prep for a surgery I've got tomorrow. Holler if you need anything."

Then she disappeared into her office, leaving the two of us in the hallway alone.

"Your mom's nice," I said to Sammy as we made our way back downstairs to join the others.

"Yeah, she's pretty great," Sammy agreed. "We're really close, you know? Totally like Lorelei and Rory on *Gilmore Girls*. Except Mom didn't have me when she was a teenager and *she's* actually the brainy one. I'm more of the wild card, if you could believe it."

I nodded. I could.

Once reunited, the four of us made plans to meet at London's house the following afternoon. He said his dad was out of town and that we'd have the place to ourselves. Well, if we weren't counting the house staff.

As I retrieved my bag from the den, Sammy offered to walk me back to the front door.

"I'm glad we were paired up," she said, leaning against the doorframe as I stood just outside her front porch. "It'll give us a chance to get to know each other better."

Super.

"Me too!" I said, hoping it didn't come off as fake.

And then I rushed off as quickly as I could before she could ask me any more questions I didn't want to answer.

Twenty minutes later, I burst into Grigg Street Pizza ready to grovel for being late. I hadn't been lying to Sammy when I'd said I needed to meet my uncle. I would've been on time, too, if he hadn't chosen our favorite pizza place for dinner, since it was so far away from Sammy's house.

I could only hope that Uncle Scotty was already elbow-deep in bubbling cheese by now. If he was, then he'd forgive me anything. Grigg Street had that effect on people.

I breathed in the smell of pizza as soon as I entered, and instantly felt at ease. We came here at least once a week, and the guys who owned the place knew us by now. They liked us because we were adventurous. We didn't get the same old thing every time. Well, *I* didn't get the same thing every time. Uncle Scotty always stuck to the ever-safe pepperoni pie, but to his credit, he always tried whatever interesting concoction the chefs had cooked up, and which I happily ordered.

I admired the decor as if it were my first time seeing it, which wasn't exactly typical of a 'za restaurant. The place had been adorned with posters from the concerts that the two owners had been to over the years, as well as with their favorite musical albums. The vibe was funky and cool, and I absolutely adored it.

I beelined for the same table that Uncle Scotty and I

always sat at. If it was taken when we arrived, we'd wait until the occupants left to sit down. There was no real reason for it. It's not like it was any more comfortable than the other tables. It was sort of just . . . tradition.

Our tradition.

Like our family dinners themselves.

I didn't look up until I was nearly at the table, trying to prolong having to see the disappointed look on my uncle's face for being late for as long as possible. But when I did finally raise my eyes, I noticed that someone was sitting in our spot.

But it wasn't Uncle Scotty.

"Kayla!" I said, surprised when I saw her. "What a weird coincidence! Two nights in a row. I'm actually meeting my uncle here for dinner. . . ."

I looked around for Uncle Scotty but didn't see him. Then I turned to the front to see if Uncle Scotty was waiting there and I just hadn't noticed. But he wasn't. So I turned back to look in the direction of the bathroom.

But he wasn't there, either. So, I turned back to Kayla again and gave her a confused smile.

"Frankie!" she said, looking happy to see me. "Hi!"

"Are you here with someone?" I asked her. "A *date*, maybe?"

I fluttered my eyes during the last bit, trying my best to look romantic but coming off as a lunatic.

"Not exactly," she said, grinning. "I'm here to meet you. Surprise!"

She shot her hands out in front of her and did a strange sort of spirit fingers motion.

"Huh?" I asked completely confused now.

Kayla gestured for me to sit down and pushed a cherry coke over as I got settled. I took a sip, even more perplexed as to how she knew what drink to order me.

"Scotty got caught up at work and asked me to come to meet you here," she explained after I placed my backpack on the floor near my feet.

"Right," I said slowly. "Work."

It wasn't that I didn't believe her. But the whole thing was a little weird considering that Uncle Scotty had never sent someone else in his place before.

"Look, I know you're bummed that you got stuck with me, but I'll try to be just as much fun as your uncle," she said.

"Wouldn't take much," I said, trying not to let my emotions show.

"So . . . how are things?" she asked, once I'd settled in.

"Uh, the same as when you asked me yesterday?" I said carefully.

I couldn't help it. This whole thing was starting to feel a little off. First Kayla stays late at our house talking to Uncle Scotty about me—which the more I thought about it, was a tad bit sneaky—and now she was overstepping by trying to act all parental and invading my personal space.

"Oh," she said. "Right. Okay. Well, how was school?"

I studied her, trying to decide if she was asking because

she was actually curious, or if Uncle Scotty had told her to.

"Same old," I said carefully.

She nodded like she was taking this in.

"Are there any cute boys in your class?" she asked, leaning in like we were girlfriends dishing our secrets. Except that, we weren't.

"Why?" I asked her, leaning in, too. "Are you looking?"

Kayla flinched.

"No," she said, shaking her head and looking horrified. "Of course not. I just thought—"

"What's going on, Kayla?" I asked bluntly.

"I told you," she said, sitting back in her seat again. "Your uncle asked me to meet you."

"Why?" I asked.

"Because he's working late," she said, like maybe I hadn't heard her the first time. Then she added, "And he didn't want you to eat dinner alone."

"But why did he send . . . *you*?"

I didn't mean it as harshly as it came out, and when I saw Kayla's face fall, I immediately I felt awful. I hadn't meant to hurt her feelings. But this whole situation was so weird, I felt thrown off guard.

"Sorry, I meant, why didn't he just text me that he'd meet me at home?" I said, trying to smooth things over. "Instead of *inconveniencing* you."

She perked up a little at my explanation.

"Hanging with you? And getting to eat Grigg Street?" she asked just as someone put two pizzas down onto the tabletop in front of us. We both breathed in deeply and smiled. "Not an inconvenience at all."

I shrugged. No matter what this was, a girl still had to eat. So I grabbed a piece of the pie that was closest and shoved it into my mouth.

"Mmmmm," I said hungrily. "Bacon and . . ."

I tried to place the other ingredient but didn't get very far.

"Roasted onion!" a man called out from the back.

"Thanks!" I yelled back. "It's pizz-awesome!"

I heard him chuckle and then I took another huge bite.

"Okay, definitely better than eating cereal at home by myself," I told Kayla, who was already on her second slice.

We ate in silence for a bit, the only sound being the music playing and our chewing.

"So, do anything fun lately?" Kayla asked me, trying once again to spark a conversation.

I made a face.

"Mostly just hang out with Ollie," I said. Then I started laughing. "If you can call Ollie fun."

"Your dad told me that—"

"My . . . *dad*?" I asked, stopping her midsentence.

Had she been talking to my dad?

How had she even known about him?

Had Uncle Scotty *actually* betrayed my trust by letting her in on who I was?

Besides that, why in the world would Dad ever talk to her? True, Kayla was nice and I didn't get the treachery vibe from her, but it didn't mean we could trust her with any of our secrets. Not this soon, at least. And what did she even want with my dad in the first place?

Warning bells were going off like fireworks vibrating through my body, making me feel queasy and off-balance. I had to get out of there.

"Sorry," Kayla said, sputtering. "I didn't mean—"

"Stop!" I yelled, standing up from my chair so quickly that it fell over with a loud clang. "Just stop!"

Kayla jumped.

I almost jumped too.

But instead, I ran.

Right out the door.

Entry Twenty-One

"You just . . . *ran*?" Ollie asked as he watched me pace around his bedroom. "All the way here?"

"Of course I didn't run *here*," I said to him. "You're like, five miles away, Ollie. I ran out the *door*."

He paused.

"And you're sure you didn't bring any pizza with you?" he asked the question like it wasn't the craziest thing he'd said that day.

I stopped walking and shot him a look.

"Okay, okay!" Ollie said, holding up his hands in surrender. Then, under his breath, he added, "You know Grigg Street is my favorite."

"Excuse me for being too busy freaking out to stop and grab leftovers for you," I said, the anger at my uncle bubbling over onto my friend.

When I saw his face, I slunk over to him and dropped down next to him on the bed. As I rolled onto my back to stare up at the ceiling, I patted his hand.

"Sorry, O," I said. "I just can't believe Uncle Scotty would betray our relationship like that."

"By sending Kayla to have dinner with you?" he asked. "Is it really that big of a deal?"

"Not *that*," I explained. "That was just . . . annoying. No, I'm ticked off because Uncle Scotty *had* to have told Kayla about my past if she knew about my dad."

Ollie sucked his breath in through his teeth. "Eeesh," he said. "Yeah, that's not good."

"And then she *talked* to him? To my *dad*?" I asked, my voice growing louder again. "What was she thinking? Who does she think she is?"

Ollie nodded.

"I haven't even talked to your dad yet," he added.

"See?" I gestured. "And I *trust* you."

"I should hope so," he said with a snort. "I'm very trustworthy. And there's the fact that I *am* your partner and all."

I reached out and patted his arm.

"That's right," I agreed.

We lay there in silence, both lost in our own thoughts.

Finally, I rolled onto my side and looked at Ollie. "So . . . that was *my* day," I said, forcing a smile. "Tell me yours was better?"

"It was, actually!" he said, brightening a bit, before scrambling to sit up. "I slayed at all my musical numbers during practice and then Mrs. Hazel offered me the part of Regina's understudy! How exciting is that?"

"Super exciting," I agreed, though I couldn't seem to match Ollie's enthusiasm. "Wait, but I thought you already have a part?"

Now it was Ollie's turn to roll his eyes.

"How are you so worldly about some stuff but so clueless about the theater?" he asked me, sounding confounded.

"Take it up with my old man," I said, throwing my hands up. "He came up with the curriculum."

Ollie shook his head.

"The understudy also learns the second part, but only steps in if something happens to the original actor," he explains.

"That could be arranged," I said grumpily.

Ollie let out a low whistle. "Now *you're* beginning to sound like Regina."

I waved him off, but then flashed a smile.

"Well, I'm proud of you, Ollie," I said. "I know you've been working hard on the musical. You deserve to have all the leads."

"All the leads?" he repeated, a dreamy look crossing his face. "Just me? A one-man show? That would be so cool!"

"Speaking of cool, I know you've been in plays with Sammy and everything, but have you ever been to her house?" I asked, changing the subject. "It's really nice. And she's got an interesting relationship with her mom."

"Oh, yeah?" Ollie asked, getting up from his bed and plodding over to his vanity. It was pristinely white and held three vertical mirrors, along with six bulbs that lit up the area like a stage. "How so?"

"They just seem to get along really well," I said.

When Ollie shot me a look in his mirror, I tried to explain it better.

"I don't know. It's like they're more friends than parent and kid? She seemed genuinely happy to see Connie when she got home," I said, like this was the oddest part of all.

"Her mom was there?" he asked, his face a blend of surprise and concern.

"Oh, yeah!" I said, realizing I'd been so distracted by the Kayla thing that I hadn't given him the rundown of what had happened during our after-school session. "So, get this: I sneak into Connie's office to search for stuff and when I'm leaving I run right into her!"

Ollie's eyes widened. "No!"

"Yes!" I said.

"What did she do?" he asked, so caught up in my story that he'd forgotten he'd just been powdering his nose.

"She said, 'hi,' " I offered grandly.

Ollie's face dropped.

"Hi?" he repeated, like he didn't believe me.

"Yep. Just 'hi,' like it wasn't weird at all that one of her daughter's friends was in her office without her permission," I said, my shock over the experience still obvious.

"Oh," Ollie said. "Sort of anticlimactic, but okay."

I nodded.

"But what I found on her computer was not," I said, a mischievous grin spreading across my face.

"Ooooh, goody!" He clapped excitedly as he hurried back over to where I sat on his bed and belly flopped down next to me. "Tell me *everything*."

I did better than that. I showed him.

"So, it's just *gone*?" Ollie asked once I'd revealed the nearly depleted bank accounts in Connie's name.

"Even *I* have more money than they do," I said, nodding.

"That's wild!" he said, shaking his head in disbelief. "What do you think happened?"

I snapped my laptop shut and traced the sticker along the cover mindlessly.

"No idea," I said. "But I'd like to find out."

"Uh-oh. What's that look for, Frankie?" Ollie asked, surprising me out of my thoughts, which had begun to wander.

"Huh?" I asked, distracted. "Oh, I'm not really sure yet."

"Yeah, right," Ollie snorted. "I've never known you to not have your mind made up about absolutely everything. What are you thinking?"

I smiled at him, because he was right. I was thinking something that I wasn't telling him. Time to say it out loud.

"It's just . . . after seeing Sammy and her mom together, and then the lack of funds bankrolling their family's lifestyle, I'm wondering if there isn't something more going on here?"

"Like what?" Ollie asked, resting his chin on his hands.

"Like, maybe that this whole admissions thing is out of necessity and not just because they feel entitled to cheat the system?" I offered slowly, still trying to work things out myself. "I've known my fair share of bad guys and they just aren't setting off any alarms."

"You think so?" Ollie asked me, surprised. "I mean, it makes sense. From what I've seen of Sammy, she's not the cheating type. So, whether her mom is or not, I don't think Sammy knows about it. She wouldn't want to win a part that way."

I nodded, as I thought this over.

"So . . . ," Ollie started.

"So . . . ," I repeated. "Maybe their lives don't deserve to be destroyed?"

The question hung in the air between us as we both thought what that meant.

"Are you saying we just scrap the whole scheme?" he asked incredulously.

"No!" I exclaimed quickly. "Not at all. I'm just wondering if maybe there's a way they can be punished where they actually just learn their lessons instead of ruining their whole futures? At least, for the ones who don't deserve it."

"Annabelle still deserves it, though, right?" Ollie asked, looking worried.

"As of right now?" I answered. "Oh, yeah."

"Okay, then I'm in," Ollie offered. "So, what's our new plan?"

I thought about this a minute.

"I think we need to find out more," I say slowly. "About everyone. Why the Faux Four are trying to game the system? How it's going to affect the kids if their parents are punished? Once we know that, we can figure out how to proceed."

"But we still proceed?" Ollie asked.

"Definitely," I said without hesitation. "Somebody has to pay for what's going on here. We just have to decide who that's going to be."

Ollie nodded in agreement

We heard a buzz across the room and Ollie jumped up to see whose phone had sprung to life. He glanced at both cells, which were still lying where we'd discarded them earlier.

"Yours!" Ollie called out, and then tossed it over his shoulder to me.

I caught it without a problem and then instantly stuck my tongue out when I saw who it was.

"My uncle," I said, without excitement.

"Oooooh, somebody's in trouble!" Ollie singsonged as he made his way back over to where I was sitting.

"Ugh," I said, shoving my phone under one of Ollie's pillows.

"Aren't you going to answer?" Ollie asked me, looking like he was in shock by the move.

"No, thank you," I said. "I don't want to hear his apologies yet."

"Maybe he's not calling to apologize?" Ollie said, pulling the phone back out and looking at its screen. "Wait, he's texting now."

"Just turn it off!" I shouted, this time choosing to bury my *head* under the pillow instead.

"He says, 'What were you thinking, Frankie? This kind of behavior is unacceptable. Get. Home. Now! Or you're grounded for the rest of your life.' "

Ollie read off the text using his best Detective Lorde voice, and while it was a bit muffled, I had to admit, it wasn't a bad impression.

"He sounds serious in this book," Ollie said, a worried look on his face once I emerged again.

"Yeah, well . . . I'm *seriously* mad," I said to him. "What he did was so wrong, I don't even know if I want to live there anymore! Maybe I'll just come and live here with you. Your room's big enough. And your mom's always saying that I barely eat anything. Nobody will even notice I'm here."

"And have your uncle come looking for you, and taking me away in handcuffs? No way," Ollie said, shaking his head emphatically.

"Don't be so dramatic," I said. "He'd totally give you a head start before he threw you in the squad car."

Ollie's face turned white. "Not funny."

I let out a strangled groan.

"I'm not going home!" I said adamantly.

Ollie looked away, but not before I saw the look on his face.

"You think I'm wrong," I stated it like it was a fact.

When he looked back around at me, I knew it was true.

"Not . . . exactly," he said, fidgeting. "More like, I think you should go home and find out his side of things."

"*His* side?" I cried out in astonishment.

"Yeah," Ollie said with a sigh. "As in, another truth besides yours. All I'm saying is that it might not be what you think."

I stared at him as I felt my world tip sideways for the second time that evening. Then I got to my feet roughly and stomped over to where I'd dropped my bag onto the floor. I threw it over my shoulder and then glanced back, my eyes squinting at my friend fiercely.

"Way to be on my side," I said angrily. "*Partner.*"

And then I stalked out.

Entry Twenty-Two

"That better be you, Frankie," Uncle Scotty yelled out, breaking the silence in our usually quiet house as I walked inside. I closed the door a little harder than was needed and tossed my bag on the floor. It was obvious that my uncle was angry. But I was angrier.

"Who else would it be?" I asked as I crossed the living room and went straight into the kitchen. "Kayla?"

As I said her name, I shot him a pointed look.

Uncle Scotty's mouth dropped open in disbelief, but he recovered quickly.

"What's gotten into you?" he asked, getting up from his favorite lounge chair and joining me in the kitchen. "Kayla told me what happened, and the way you treated her—well, it wasn't okay."

I grabbed a soda from the fridge and then slammed it onto the counter, making Uncle Scotty flinch.

"You know what's not okay?" I said to him, narrowing my eyes. "Telling people about Dad."

His face scrunched up in confusion.

"What are you talking about?" he asked, shaking his head.

"Don't play dumb, Uncle Scotty. It's not a good look

on you," I warned. Then I added, "So much for our rule of never lying to each other."

I ignored the fact that I'd lied to him on several occasions myself. But he was the adult, and it had been *his* rule. You couldn't break your own rule.

"I've never lied to you, Frankie," he said softly. "Especially about your dad."

I snorted in response.

"Let's start over," he suggested, calmer now. "What happened tonight? Kayla said you were kind of brusque with her, and then you yelled at her and ran out?"

"What happened was that you ditched me for dinner and then sent Kayla in to babysit me," I said. "And then you told her all about me and Dad without even asking if it was okay. But worst of all, she actually *talked* to him."

Uncle Scotty closed his eyes for a second and when he opened them again, there was a look in his eyes that made my mouth go dry. It was all the confirmation I needed, and I immediately snatched up my drink and fled to the safety and solace of my bedroom. Once inside, I threw myself onto my bed and tried not to cry.

"Frankie?" a voice called softly. Uncle Scotty had obviously followed me upstairs and was now standing at my door. "Can I come in?"

I didn't raise my head.

"It's your house," I said, my voice muffled by the pillows. "You can do whatever you want."

"But it's your room," he responded. "And I respect your privacy and your space."

"Are you kidding me?" I bellowed.

"Now wait a minute," Uncle Scotty said, trying his best to be patient and composed. "Let's get this figured out here. About tonight: I thought you liked Kayla. Do you not?"

I turned my face to the side so I could still breathe, but not be visible to my uncle.

"I *did* like Kayla," I said carefully. "I liked her a lot. But then you started pushing her on me and now she's butting into my business, and well, I'm over it."

"First off, I wasn't trying to force her on you or anything like that," he explained. "It's just, she's the only adult I've ever heard you talk about with any kind of fondness. Well, except for your dad. And when I knew I wasn't going to make it to dinner, I thought she'd be the perfect person to join you. You had so much fun working with her at The Farm and I figured you could catch up. Obviously, I was wrong."

"You think?" I said, still worked up, but feeling my emotions start to wane a bit.

"I'm trying to be understanding here, Frankie, but you're making it kind of hard," he said, firmly. "Now, I'm sorry for canceling. And I'm sorry I didn't ask you about Kayla, even though I genuinely thought you'd have fun. It was my mistake and it won't happen again. But I don't know what you're talking about regarding your dad."

I turned over so I was facing him again and saw

that he was still standing in my doorway. He hadn't moved inside because I hadn't told him he could. He was obviously trying to respect my boundaries. I just wish he'd done it earlier.

"You don't have to stand there," I muttered. "You can come in."

"Okay," he said, walking inside and sitting down at my desk. "So, why do you think I told Kayla about your dad?"

"Because she told me you did," I said.

Uncle Scotty frowned.

"That can't be right," he said, out loud but mostly to himself. Then he turned his eyes on me. "Frankie, I haven't said anything about your dad to anyone. Not even to people I'm close to. That's your story to tell."

"Well, somebody told her and it wasn't me," I said.

"And I'm telling you, it wasn't me, either," he said.

I looked into his eyes and my convictions instantly began to waver. He'd never flat out lied to me before and my gut was telling me he wasn't now. So, what the heck was going on then?

"Do you mind if I do a little detective work here?" he asked.

I raised an eyebrow skeptically, but finally nodded.

Then he took out his phone and started to type on it furiously.

A few seconds later, there was a loud bell sound, signaling he had a new message.

"Ooooooh!" he said, understanding crossing his face as he finished reading.

Then he tossed his cell over to me so I could read what it said. I did so, reluctantly.

Did you mention Frankie's dad to her?

Yes, but only by mistake. I accidentally called YOU her "dad" instead of her "uncle." By the time I realized what I'd said, she was already gone.

Oh, no! Is that why she ran out? We've never even talked about her dad before.

Gotcha. It was a simple mistake. Frankie's just a private person and when you said that, she thought we'd been talking about her behind her back.

Oh my goodness! No! Is she really upset? Should I come by and talk to her about it? Explain things?

Nah. We're working it out now. Everything will be fine.

Sorry, Scotty.

No worries. I'll text you later.

As I read the text chain, I felt the fire that had been burning in me fizzle out. I'd totally freaked out for no reason. And I'd been kind of awful to Kayla in the process.

I could feel Uncle Scotty watching me, but I didn't dare look up at him. I was too embarrassed. I'd created too much drama. Falsely accused both of them of things they hadn't done.

"I thought—" I started but couldn't get myself to finish.

"Let's just chalk this up to a bad day of misinformation," Uncle Scotty chimed in, saving me from myself.

I nodded in agreement.

"I *do* think we can learn from all this though," he added carefully. "We could all stand to be a little better at communicating—myself included. And that's why I want to talk to you about something."

I looked up at him surprised to hear this. I couldn't help it. A sense of foreboding flooded my system.

"Er, I know you've been wondering why Kayla's suddenly been coming around here. And while, it *is* a hundred percent true that she missed you and Geronimo, and cares about you guys . . ."

He paused here, trying to choose his next words wisely.

I sat there waiting for the other shoe to drop.

And then it did.

". . . she also cares about me," he said quickly. "And I care about her. I guess what I'm trying to say is we're sort of dating?"

I blinked at him.

"I'm sorry," I said. "I think I just hallucinated. What did you say?"

Uncle Scotty gave me an exasperated look.

"I'm dating Kayla," he repeated.

"What?" I asked, stunned by the information.

"Don't make me say it again, Frankie," Uncle Scotty said, running his hand down his face.

"Okay," I said, feeling my frustration rising again. "And when were you planning on telling me?"

Now it was Uncle Scotty's turn to look surprised.

"Well, I suppose whenever I felt like there was something to tell," he answered truthfully. "It wasn't until recently that we decided this actually *was* something. That *we* were something."

I shook my head.

"I can't believe this," I said quietly.

"I know. We were pretty surprised when it happened ourselves—"

"No," I said, staring straight at him. "I can't believe you made this decision without me."

"I love you, Frankie, but don't you think this is a decision for me and Kayla to make?" he asked.

"I think that when your decision affects me and my life that I should have a say in it too," I argued.

"Frankie—"

"You know, I didn't have a choice when Dad decided not to run that day in Paris. He thought it was the best decision for me and now I'm paying for it. I'm sick of adults thinking they're the only ones whose opinions matter," I said, punching my fist into one of my pillows. "Shouldn't what I want matter too? Or is this your world and I'm just living in it?"

"Wow," Uncle Scotty said, staring at me hard. For once, I couldn't read him. I got the sense that I might've gone too far, but I didn't care.

My dad had made a decision that changed my future. The Faux Four were in the middle of making choices that would forever impact their kids' lives. And now Uncle Scotty was deciding what was best for the two of us.

It wasn't fair. And I wasn't going to go quietly.

"I just want to be alone now," I said, turning and lying down with my back to him again.

I waited until I could hear the swishing of his pants and then my door shut before I rolled onto my back to stare up at the ceiling.

Worst. Day. Ever.

Entry Twenty-Three

"So, I think we've pretty much established that the guy was a total creep," London said, lounging inside an egg-like chair that hung from his ceiling.

Sammy, Benji, and I had gone home with London after school that day to continue the work on our project. We'd officially decided to tackle the biggest of the #MeToo scandals in class that day, our substitute giving us the go-ahead almost immediately.

So, after school, his personal driver had picked us up, happily helping us up into a massive black SUV with tinted windows. Inside were different-colored LED lights, giving off a club kind of vibe.

The four of us had listened to music along the way, each person taking a turn in choosing a song. The mix of tunes was all over the place. I'd, of course, chosen an old-school classic from the band Queen. Sammy had picked a Norah Jones hit. London had surprised us all by choosing country crooner Dierks Bentley. We'd arrived at London's before Benji got his chance to pick a tune, but I'd looked back at him during the drive once or twice and he hadn't even been bobbing his head to the music. He just stared out the window silently.

But once we arrived at London's, I forgot all about that.

The Max's estate—and that's what it was—was a Japanese-inspired behemoth that consisted of three tiered, flat levels of house. The back was almost entirely windows, with a whole area opening the living room and kitchen up to the outside. It was clean and bright, but with a masculine vibe. All the furniture was boxy and angular, and the color scheme was black, white, and tan wood. It was obvious that a woman didn't live there. The bones of the house were just too frosty.

London had led us right into his "chill room"—what most would call a den—and we'd all made ourselves comfortable as if we'd been there a hundred times before. That was the weird thing about this group. It felt really *comfortable* being around each other. Like, we were all cut from the mold in a way.

Or maybe like we were all damaged whether we realized it or not.

Then again, maybe it was just the fact that the others had all known one another for what seemed like forever, their parents being besties long before their kids were ever born.

Still, even as the outsider, I felt like I fit in with them. This, of course, was weird in and of itself, but I decided to go with it. Especially since it could only help my recon.

"Most Hollywood execs are creeps though, right? So what was it about that one big guy who was called out that was different?" I asked, taking a sip of sparkling water. "Do you think he just assumed he was untouchable because he was rich and powerful?"

There was a minifridge in the corner that held every kind of drink you could think of. And on a nearby countertop was an assortment of snacks all perfectly organized. I bet it was restocked every day. And then there was a pillow in the middle of the room that was the size of a bed. It felt like clouds.

Somebody could've lived in this room and never have to leave. I could live in this room.

Maybe I'd just stay here instead of going home. The place was so big, I bet nobody would even notice me. And then I wouldn't have to deal with the fallout after my fight with Uncle Scotty.

We hadn't talked since the night before when I'd asked him to leave my room. This morning I lay awake in my bed until I could hear him in the shower and then I got dressed as quickly as I could, scrawled a note on the chalkboard in the kitchen that said *Went to school early*, and then took off. I'd avoided Ollie by eating solo in the library, while simultaneously doing some additional research into the Faux Four.

And now I was spending my afternoon with the kids of my current marks.

"I think that anyone who has that much money and power can start to believe they can do anything they want," London said, looking over at a Superman poster hanging on the wall. "People like that are also not used to being told no. It can be a scary combo when they're not opposed to using their powers for evil."

In the poster the superhero was standing front and center, arms in the super-stance he was known for. Flanked on either side of him was a beautiful, dark-haired girl and a bald man wearing an expensive suit. I was still looking at the superhero poster when I suddenly realized that the man playing the unitard-wearing caped crusader was Dakota. I snuck a glance back at London and wondered if his earlier reference had been meant for Lex Luther or his dad.

Maybe hanging in London's house to avoid everything that was going on with Uncle Scotty and Kayla wasn't the greatest idea after all. My Spidey senses were tingling—which I realized was a totally different superhero reference, but it seemed appropriate anyway—and that usually meant trouble was in the air.

And I definitely didn't need any more trouble.

"Earth to Frankie!" Sammy called out, suddenly waving her hand right in front of my face.

"Oh!" I said, startled out of my thoughts. "Sorry. I was just thinking."

"Not about the project, I take it?" she answered with a smile.

I smiled back, sheepishly.

"Sorry," I offered.

"Come on," Sammy said. "Spill."

"But we've got work to do," I argued. "We don't have time for my stuff."

"Sure, we do," she said. "Besides, we could use the break."

"And a distraction from our own complicated lives," London said unenthusiastically.

I raised an eyebrow at this, but inside I couldn't believe the amazing opening they'd given me. I'd been looking for a way to get them talking and here it was. All I had to do was give them a piece of myself, first.

I could do that.

Just make something up that would make them think we were the same. That they could open up to me. Tell me their secrets without revealing any of mine.

"I just found out that my uncle is . . . *dating*," I blurted out.

And then I'd gone and told them the truth.

I had no idea why I did it. Maybe it was because I was still mad at Ollie and couldn't talk to him about what had happened. Maybe it was because I didn't feel like having to make up yet another story.

Or maybe I had a feeling that they'd understand.

No matter why I'd done it, it was too late now. Besides, what would be the harm in telling them?

"And you're really protective of your uncle?" London asked slowly, like he was confused.

I shook my head.

"Sorry, I guess you sort of need some background to get it," I said. "I live with my uncle. That's why I moved here. Because my dad's—well, he's out of the picture.

Anyway, my uncle just told me that he's been dating this woman and I had no idea."

"Let me guess," Sammy said. "She's a total nightmare?"

I looked over at her in surprise.

"Not at all," I said, carefully. "Actually, she's really cool as far as adults go. She's the kind of person who never treats a kid like, well, a kid. And she's nice. Like super nice. And funny."

"And you don't like funny people," London said seriously.

When he broke out into a silly smile, I rolled my eyes.

"Okay, fine!" I exclaimed. "I get that it sounds weird. Here's this perfect girl and all I can do is complain."

"So, what's the actual problem?" London asked, crossing his arms over his chest and placing his hands under his armpits.

"I suppose the problem is that my uncle never *told* me he wanted to date her," I shared. "He just did it and thought I'd be okay with it."

"I gotta say," London said, scrunching up his face, "I don't think in my entire time living with Dakota, that he has ever asked me my opinion on anything. Even the kind of cereal we keep in the house."

I shook my head.

"But doesn't that make you mad?" I asked him, hopping up from my spot on the ginormous pillow.

He shrugged. "It is what it is."

"But it shouldn't be!" I complained.

"Hey, I'd be more than peeved to find out my mom

was dating," Sammy agreed. But then she winked at me. "Of course my mom's married to my dad so that would be a whole other thing."

"It's not the fact that he's dating!" I said, throwing my arms up in the air.

"It's the fact that he's not even asking how you *feel* about it," Benji said, shocking all of us as he spoke. Sammy even jumped a little, before settling back into her chair.

I studied Benji closely. I'd never noticed how deep his voice was before. Then again, maybe it was just that he so rarely talked that it hadn't ever registered.

He was still staring at me, not the least bit uncomfortable by the prolonged eye contact. But I was starting to be. It felt like he was somehow going to be able to read my mind.

Or look into my soul.

Finally, I was the one who looked away.

"Exactly," I said, agreeing with his earlier assessment. "It's like, here he is making decisions that are going to directly impact my life and he doesn't even think that I deserve to be a part of the process."

"Right," London said, sitting up straighter now. He pulled at his lower lip absently. "I get that. Dakota is set on me playing sports. He keeps hinting he wants me to go to a different school—one that focuses on athletics instead of academics. But I'm just not into it."

"Aren't you on like, three sports teams, though?" I asked. I hadn't actually known this until I'd done research on him. I wasn't exactly a joiner, either, and sports were definitely a joiner activity.

London shrugged. "Yeah, but just because I'm good at them doesn't mean I like it," he answered.

I nodded, but I never would've thought that there were people out there who didn't like what they were good at. Wasn't that part of liking what you did? That you were good at it? I figured that the two were synonymous.

"Have you tried telling him?" I asked.

London and Sammy looked at each other and laughed.

"What?" I asked, looking over at Benji like he was going to clue me in. But even he was smiling.

"I've told him like a trillion times," London said, still chuckling. "Dude doesn't listen. If you knew Dakota, you'd understand. He gets his mind set on something then that's it. End game."

"But if you're miserable—"

"He doesn't care," London said bluntly. "My being an athlete just adds to the narrative he's trying to create for himself. Successful celebrity adopts orphan. Kid becomes famous athlete. He doesn't really have an imagination in that way."

I closed my mouth, not sure what to say to that.

"It's okay," London said then, with a wave. "Well, it's not okay, but I'm used to it. It's like you were saying, parents make decisions for us all the time. Even if they're not the ones we'd make for ourselves."

I shook my head.

"But it shouldn't be that way," I said. Then I seemed to

suddenly remember why I had concocted this whole project in the first place. "Are your parents the same way?"

I looked over at Benji and then at Sammy expectantly.

"Well, my mom is the best. She's pretty much my best friend," Sammy said.

"And that's why we hate you," London said, but we could all tell he was joking.

"I'm aware," Sammy responded before moving on. "But I *do* wish she wouldn't work so much. She's always telling me that she works so she can give me everything her parents couldn't. She wants me to be able to go anywhere I want and be anything I want, without the worry of money. But I just don't care about money that much."

"I bet you'd care just a little if you couldn't go to that fancy theater camp every summer, or you had to give up that famous acting coach you have on speed dial," London said with a nod.

"I wasn't saying that all that wasn't nice," Sammy agreed. "But honestly, I'd give it all up just to have Mom home more often. I've told her that before, but she doesn't seem to care."

"At least she cares enough to know what you're into," Benji said, making us all look over at him now. "My mom's so focused on my brother Cassius being a screwup, that I'm pretty sure she doesn't even know I exist. A few years ago, Cass told me I was a ghost, and I actually believed him since rarely anyone ever talks to me."

Sammy walked over to Benji and put her hand on

his shoulder and squeezed. "That's ridiculous, Benji," she said seriously. "I mean, if you *were* a ghost, why would you want to haunt them? I mean, choose somebody more exciting, like Beyoncé or one of the Kardashians."

This made all of us laugh, even Benji.

"In all seriousness though," London said once we'd calmed down. "Your brother's a turd. And your mom . . . well, I'm not going to talk bad about anybody's mama, but she's never had her priorities straight. Even when we were all babies, she seemed to care more about what people thought of your family rather than whether her family was happy."

Benji just nodded, but his frown had become just a little bit less sad. In fact, he almost appeared . . . relieved? Like it felt good to know other people saw and understood his pain.

"Maybe that's why Dakota gets along with your mom so well, Benji," London added after a brief pause. "He's all about appearances too. Why do you think he adopted me? A good-looking, super-talented black kid from the streets. There's no better PR than that."

I was taking a sip of my drink as he said this and nearly choked on it.

"Okay, okay," Sammy said, walking over and clapping me on the back. "Let's not scare away the new girl. We could use a little normal in this group."

The fact that anyone thought that I was normal was enough to make me choke again.

Entry Twenty-Four

"Your dad's on the phone," Uncle Scotty said later that night. "You up for a talk?"

I scrambled off my bed and rushed over to where Uncle Scotty was standing just outside the door, again. He really never came in unless I invited him in. I'd mentioned to him once that those were the rules of a vampire, too, and he'd joked that maybe he was a bloodsucker from beyond the grave. Then I'd told him that it was unlikely since he wouldn't even eat steak if it had a bit of pink to it.

But now his lingering just felt passive aggressive and annoying.

I snatched the phone out of his hand and ran back over to my bed where I flopped down onto my stomach with my back to him. I waited until I heard the door close and then placed the phone to my ear.

"Dad?"

"Frankie, baby!" he said, sounding over-the-top chipper for somebody who spent his days in a six-foot cell with a guy named Sparky.

My excitement to talk to him gave way to worry as I remembered where he was calling me from, and that this wasn't his usual day to call.

"What's up?" I said immediately, butterflies kicking up in my stomach.

"Now why would anything be wrong?" Dad said.

"Um, because you're calling from *prison*!" I exclaimed, rolling my eyes even though he couldn't see me.

"Nothing's wrong, Frankie," he insisted. "You've really gotta start thinking more positively."

"Because life has never let me down before?" I answered sarcastically.

"Right," Dad said with a laugh. "It has to get better from here."

"I'm not sure that's how it works," I said, but let it go. "So, what's up? Why the surprise check-in?"

"Can't a dad call his only daughter just to see how she's doing?" he said.

"A dad can," I agreed. "You, however, don't. So, what is it? Spill."

"All right. Sometimes I forget that you're my daughter and would never fall for this stuff," he muttered.

I smiled.

"Scotty called me," he admitted. "Said you might need to talk."

I groaned. "Of course he did," I said, not bothering to hide my frustration. "So, what did he tell you?"

"Nothing specific," he said. "Just that I might wanna call."

"That's cryptic," I noted. "Doesn't that bug you?"

"Maybe a little," he admitted. "But then I remind

myself that he's just trying to do right by you by not telling your business to anyone."

"Wow," I said in a mock serious tone. "Prison's changed you."

He laughed heartily.

"I know, right?"

I could practically picture him where he was, leaning up against the wall, one leg casually crossed over the other at the ankle. It was the same stance Uncle Scotty had when he was standing around.

"So, spill it, kid," he said, finally.

"There have to be more important things to talk about than this," I argued, both wanting to tell him everything and not wanting to bring it up at all.

"Nothing is more important than you," he said, suddenly serious.

"Fine," I said, giving in. "Uncle Scotty's got a girlfriend. Did he tell you that?"

There was a pause on the other line.

"No. He did not," he answered.

"Well, he does," I said.

"Okay," he responded. "And that's a problem because . . . she's awful? Mean? A vegetarian?"

"No," I said, feeling a little déjà vu-ey over my conversation with the Faux Four kids from earlier. But I pushed forward. "No, she's really nice. Ollie and I volunteered at her animal rescue over the winter. I got Geronimo from her."

"So, why are you giving him such a hard time about it?" he asked.

"Be*cause*," I said, sharply. "He didn't ask me if it was okay to bring her into our lives."

My dad's end of the line went silent.

"Are you still there?" I asked, worried he'd run out of time.

"I'm here," he responded. "I'm just trying to figure out why you think he needs to your permission to date. He's the adult and you're the kid. Albeit, you're *my* kid and therefor superior to all others—but you're still a kid."

"Yeah, but—"

"And I shouldn't have to remind you that he opened up his home and life to you without hesitation, after I was sent away," Dad continued. "Just because you're living there, doesn't mean he should have to stop his life for you."

"I wasn't saying that—" I protested. "I'm just sick of people making decisions that alter my life so completely."

"Ahhhh," my dad said knowingly. "So, this is actually about me, and the fact that I'm in here."

"Not everything's about you, Dad," I said.

"Since when?" he joked.

We both knew that most of my life had been spent hiding in his shadow. And he was sort of right. As infamous as he was, the majority of situations that had to do with me, really *were* about him.

"Look, Franks, Scotty's just making the best decisions he can at the time he has to make them. And I can promise you without a doubt, that he always has your happiness and safety in mind."

"Well, if that's true, shouldn't he just include me in his decisions?" I asked, still wanting to argue.

"Aw, sweet girl," he began. "Sometimes a parent has to decide some things on their own."

"And I just have to be okay with that?" I asked, incredulous.

"No," Dad said. "But it would be easier for both of you if you got on board. Especially with this. And if I'm being honest, it sounds like she's pretty great."

"That's not the point," I say.

"Shouldn't it be, though?" he asked gently. "Bottom line, Frankie? Your feelings are your own. You're certainly entitled to them and they're not wrong. But I want you to ask yourself one thing: Do you want Scotty to be happy? If you do, then maybe you let this go. Or at the very least, let him know you're cool with the two of them together, just not the way he went about it. You know, keeping you in the dark and all."

He was right. When he put it that way, of course he was right. I wasn't upset because Uncle Scotty's decision was the wrong one. I was mad because he'd kept it from me. And that felt too much like a betrayal, despite the fact that Uncle Scotty would never do anything to hurt me.

When I didn't argue with him, he knew he had me. To his credit, Dad had always known when to stop pushing.

Go too far and I'd dig my heels in until they were like concrete blocks.

So, he changed the subject.

"What else is going on?" he asked. "Got any special *projects* you're working on?"

This was obviously code for: *Was I working any jobs*?

"Actually, yeah," I said. "But this one's been a challenge."

"Finally take on too much work?" he asked.

"Kind of," I said slowly, trying to figure out how to keep up the charade for whoever else was listening in on our conversation. My dad hadn't needed to tell me that someone was always monitoring our calls for me to know it was true. There was no privacy in prison. "I have tests in four classes coming up and I'm not sure I should've signed up for the subjects in the first place."

"Whoa," he said, whistling low. "That's a lot of *exams* all at once. Maybe you can ask your teachers to space them out, so you can focus on just one subject at a time?"

"That's not the problem," I said. "I'm actually more worried that if I do too well on the tests, then it will impact the other kids in my class negatively. Like, if I succeed, then they'll fail because I'll be setting the curve. Does that make sense?"

"Hmmm," Dad responded. "That *is* tough. You know, I think you're pretty amazing to be thinking about your classmates at all. Most people in your situation would only be thinking of themselves."

"Well, I was," I said honestly. "But I've started to get to know the kids in my classes and they're pretty great. Their parents are questionable, but why should they be punished for that, right?"

"Right," he answered. "I mean, not everyone's as awesome as I am."

I snorted.

"Exactly," I said sarcastically.

"So, what are you going to do?" he asked.

"Well, there *is* one more option," I said, flipping over onto my back so I was staring up at the ceiling. "Instead of taking all four tests individually and bringing down the curve, I could take one big comprehensive test that covers all four subjects. There's a school counselor type of guy who doesn't want me to go this route though, because then it'll make his job obsolete."

"Do you care what happens to him?" Dad asked.

"Not even a little bit," I said. "He sucks."

Dad laughed. "Okay. Well, it sounds like you already know what you want to do, but that you want to be told that it's the *right* thing to do."

"Is it?"

"I can't tell you that," he finished. "Only you can decide."

I threw up my hands in frustration, causing the phone to fall away from my face and land on the bed next to me.

"Well, what good are you then?" I called out, hoping he could still hear me.

"No good!" I heard him yell back as I grabbed the phone back up again.

"That's for sure," I said to him. "Now on to *you*. How are you doing?"

"Oh, I'm good," he answered with little hesitation. "I'm thinking of getting my degree while I'm in here."

"In what?" I asked, surprised by the news. Not because I didn't think he could hack it. But because he'd never been a fan of organized education.

"Criminal justice," he said.

I burst out laughing.

"You're kidding!" I shouted, unable to hide my glee.

"I'm not!" he said.

"Isn't that sort of . . . *counterproductive*?" I asked curiously.

"I like to think of it as becoming a scholar in my field of interest," he said, a hoity-toity sound to his voice. "But also, it'll be a heck of a lot easier to do my job if I understand how they do theirs."

Theirs, meaning the Feds.

"Fair enough," I said. "In that case, maybe I'll become a cop when I grow up."

"Don't you dare!" he said, sounding appalled.

Entry Twenty-Five

Plans had changed.

My talk with Dad had made two things clear:

One, I needed to make up with Uncle Scotty.

And two, I was certain now that I couldn't take down the Faux Four. Well, three of them, for sure anyway. Oh, I would still teach them a lesson—one that I hoped would make things better for the kids they were failing. But my focus was no longer on taking their money and turning them over to the authorities.

I'd gone back and forth the entire night on whether or not to include Annabelle's dad in my new "off-limits" list. There was no question Annabelle was awful, and I definitely wanted her punished for the things she'd done to me and everyone else at Western. But was destroying her whole life the way to go about it?

That was when I remembered I had something in my possession that could help me decide.

I hadn't opened Annabelle's diary since I'd taken it off her bed that first night at her house. And to be honest, with everything else going on, it had been low on my priority list. But now . . .

Now it was time to do a little light reading.

So, I'd pulled the book that held all Annabelle's private thoughts out of the same hiding place I kept my journals (this one included) and began to read.

And it changed everything.

Well, not *everything*. But enough.

Dearest Diary,

Daddy lied to me again today. We were supposed to have a special solo night out—he'd promised to take me into the city for dinner and a show—but when I got home after school, there was a note on the fridge that said he'd have to take a rain check. But the thing is, THIS was our rain check! And he hadn't even taken the time to write the note himself. By now I can tell Esmerelda's handwriting. She's been working for us for more than a decade now, and it's as recognizable to me as my own signature.

Daddy said it was because something came up at work, but I know it wasn't. I heard Esmerelda tell the chef not to prepare plates for him or Arabella because they were meeting friends out for dinner.

Why would he lie to me? And why is dinner with Arabella more important than spending time with me?

What did I do wrong?

—Annabelle

Dearest Diary,

Daddy likes Clara more than he likes me. He makes it so obvious, too. Always saying how Clara's so smart and so pretty and she always follows the rules. When I do something less-than-perfect he'll say, "Clara would have won that contest," or "Clara always got As in math."

And Clara doesn't even care what Daddy thinks! She's always avoiding him. She turns down every invitation to do something with him. I would give ANYTHING to have him pay attention to me the way he does to her. It's not fair.

She doesn't deserve it.

I do.

Why can't he see that I'm trying to be what he wants me to be?

—Annabelle

Dearest Diary,

If my own father doesn't even love me, how will anyone else? What if I'm alone forever?

I have Gladace and Penny, but I know they're only friends with me because they're scared of me.

I feel like you're the only one I can really talk to.

—Annabelle

They were all like this. Accounts of all the ways she was a disappointment to her dad. Pleas for him to pay attention to her. The lack of love she felt at home.

It was depressingly difficult to read, and incredibly frustrating at the same time, because there was no way I could ruin her now.

She was already broken.

And that's why Annabelle's diary found its way into her locker the next morning, nobody outside of the two of us privy to its contents.

This also meant that all the Faux Four were off-limits now. Which was fine, I guessed, since I'd already begun to formulate a plan with my new mark in mind.

I wanted to go after the kingpin.

The one who was making it possible for the rich to bypass lawful channels and get what they wanted at any cost. And not just in Greenwich. Across the country, most likely. Take out the king and you ended his whole reign of terror.

And to do this, I needed to get close enough for him to trust me.

I needed to be one of his potential clients.

I needed to be . . . my dad.

I'd seen how Mr. Admissions had treated the guys in the Faux Four versus the women. It had been clear that he had less respect for women. I mean, he'd practically laughed off Lily's questions. In fact I got the feeling that if Brooks hadn't been the one to set up their meeting, it never would've taken place.

So, I needed to be a guy for this next part. . . .

No biggie.

Actually, this might've been the easiest bit of the con to figure out and execute. Because there were plenty of guys to pick from.

Well, guys' voices, anyway.

Should I go deep and ominous like Morgan Freeman? Or youthful and friendly à la Tom Hanks? In the end, I chose to adopt one of the legends of voices: Seth MacFarlane.

Finding an old clip of the actor when he'd hosted *Saturday Night Live*, I recorded it with June's gadget plugged into my phone. When it had enough of a sample, I lifted it up to my mouth and gave it a try.

The change in my voice was both astonishing and a bit creepy at the same time. It sounded nothing like me.

It was perfect.

I dialed Mr. Admissions's phone number. It hadn't been difficult to find since he'd mentioned the name of the fake company he hid his dirty dealings behind during his meeting with the Faux Four.

Three rings later, I was surprised to find that it was Mr. Admissions himself who answered.

"Hello?" he said unceremoniously.

"Mr. Admissions?" Seth MacFarlane's voice echoed through the phone and to my mark.

"Clearly you know who I am," he said in response. "But who am I talking to?"

"My name is Brian MacFarlane and I was told you have a talent for getting kids into schools," I said, trying to deliver the words as confidently as I could.

There was a slight pause on the other end.

"And who told you this story?" he asked.

"Dakota Max is a buddy of mine," I replied. "We run in the same circles."

"Dakota, huh?" Mr. Admissions said, like he still wasn't sure whether to trust me or not.

"Yeah," I continued. "He told me you guys met recently at Brooks Valera's place? To discuss your *unique connections* in the academic world. Do I have the wrong guy?"

There was no hesitation this time.

"Oh, you've definitely got the right guy," he said, the arrogance loud and clear. "I'm Mr. Admissions."

"Fantastic," I said quickly. "I want my kid to go to Carington Private. No bull—can you make that happen?"

Mr. Admissions let out a loud whistle and then clucked his tongue like he was thinking it over.

"You're in luck because I know one of the administrators there and he happens to owe me a favor," Mr. Admissions said. "But you know that's one of the top schools on the East Coast, right? It's nearly impenetrable. It's going to cost you."

"Money isn't an object," I heard Daddy MacFarlane say. "Get my boy in there and you can have whatever you want."

"Wonderful," Mr. Admissions said. "Let's get started, shall we?"

And then he gave me almost an identical pitch to the one he'd given the Faux Four. He had connections. He could get kids in through the side door. I could do it on my own, but why would I want to do all that work?

I told him I was in and asked what came next.

That's when Mr. Admissions surprised me.

"Before we can go any further, I ask each of my clients the same question," he said carefully. "Why do you need my help? In other words, why can't your son get in on his own merits?"

The question took me aback. Why did he care as long as he was getting paid?

"Look, I can tell by your silence that the answer makes you uncomfortable. But I assure you, every single family I work with has answered the same question," Mr. Admissions said. "I need to know what I'm getting myself into. How to frame things for the admissions process. Better for me to know all your secrets up front than be blindsided by them when it counts. I also need some . . . insurance that this will stay between us."

There it was. The thing that was possibly even more valuable than his fee. I instantly wondered what the Faux Four had divulged. Whether Mr. Admissions was now privy to why Sammy's family was broke.

"You want the truth?" I said, trying to come up with a suitable answer for him on a limited amount of time.

"I do," he replied.

Think, think, think. Then I had it.

"What can I say? The boy is dumb as rocks."

Mr. Admissions startled me by suddenly laughing out loud.

"You have no idea how often I hear that," he said. "Okay, I'm going to need to meet with you in person to collect my fee."

"Impossible," Daddy MacFarlane said. "I'm leaving for Hong Kong later this afternoon. Perhaps my son can bring it by your house? I've already told him what's going on, so it won't be a problem for him to stop by."

"Well, I usually prefer to meet my clients *before* I take on a case," Mr. Admissions said, his voice trailing off like he was mulling this over. "But I suppose I can wave our initial consultation until you're back in town."

"Brilliant!" I said. "Now, for that fee . . ."

Entry Twenty-Six

It wasn't my first time being a boy. And unlike Ollie, I was actually very cute as the opposite sex. Luckily, gender and identity was fluid these days, so nobody would question my appearance too much.

I'd stuffed a short black wig, a hat, long basketball shorts, and an oversize Nike shirt into my school bag before I'd left the house that morning. The grocery store near school was a perfect place to change, since nobody paid attention to who was going in or out of the bathrooms that were located all the way in the back.

Not that it mattered. Nobody would've recognized me in this getup, with my hat pulled low over my forehead and the black hair of my wig sticking out from underneath.

At around three fifteen, I hopped into an Uber, which I ordered using a burner phone, and readied myself for what I was about to do.

I'd expected Mr. Admissions's house to be nice, given how much he was charging Daddy MacFarlane to get his kid into the prestigious boarding school I'd picked from my Internet search.

But what I saw when I'd finally walked up to the

address I'd been given over the phone—well, let's just say I was completely unprepared for it.

Because the thing had a freaking moat!

I didn't see it at first, since the entire estate had a wall around it and hid it from view of the main road. But once I walked up to the wrought iron gate and buzzed the intercom, I could clearly see that what lay beyond it was a bridge that extended about twenty feet across, and was wide enough for a single car. The other side of the bridge connected with the house's circular car park.

The intercom system crackled to life as I nearly pressed the button a second time.

"Hello?" came Mr. Admissions's voice, as loud as if he were actually trying to yell at me all the way from the house and not through the speaker on his end.

"Hey," I said in my boy voice. "It's Matthew MacFarlane. My dad sent me with a package to give you."

"Right," he replied, like he'd forgotten all about the meeting. "Okay, come on in."

The gate buzzed loudly beside me and then began to open, allowing me to see what else was hidden behind its walls. Thankfully, I was wearing basketball shoes as a part of my disguise, because the bridge to the house was cobblestone. This meant that every step I took was off-balance and I had to keep my eyes downcast to make sure I didn't trip.

Although I hadn't seen any cameras at the gates, I saw at least six of them now, and had to assume Mr. Admissions was watching me walk up. And the last thing

I needed was to have to explain to him why my hair fell off as I tripped on one of his stupid stones.

There were no railings on either side of the bridge. Just concrete bumpers to keep cars from going over the edge. I forced myself from the middle of the path so I could look down into the water below.

This was when I realized that it wasn't a moat at all. It was a swimming pool. A single lane that wound around the entire property, trapping the house on its own little private island. Spanning about ten feet across, the water inside was pristinely clean, reflecting brightly off the turquoise color of the tiles within.

I lifted my eyes to the house looming before me and found it to be just as impressive as its entrance. Keeping with the whole cobblestone motif, the house was three stories tall and covered completely with a mixture of stone and ivy. Large arched windows let in plenty of natural light and an eight-foot tunnel leading to the front door made it feel like you were walking into another world.

The whole place had a modern castle type of feel, and I had to admit I'd never seen anything like it.

As I walked toward the tunnel, I could see a figure emerging from the darkness of its depths. I recognized Mr. Admissions almost immediately. His long, lanky body and jerky movements made me think of the Tin Man from *The Wizard of Oz*. His silver hair even gave off the appearance of the character's funnel hat.

"Matthew MacFarlane?" Mr. Admissions asked,

meeting me just at the entrance to the tunnel and holding out his hand for me to shake.

Who else would I be? I literally just buzzed you.

But I took his hand and pumped it hard, giving it a harder squeeze than I usually would as myself.

"Cool house," I said, trying to sound both impressed and bored at the same time. Then I nodded my head in the direction of the pool moat. "You a king or something?"

Mr. Admissions let out a loud, barking laugh.

"Something like that," he answered, and then walked me over to the edge of the pool. I followed him and then looked back down into its crystal clear water. It was far too cold to swim this time of the year, but I could see how it would be refreshing during the hot summer months. Or if it was heated.

"Actually, I've been an avid swimmer ever since I was about your age. Maybe even younger. How old are you again? Fourteen? Fifteen?" he said, not bothering to wait for an answer. "Went to University of Notre Dame on a swim scholarship. Tried coaching for a while, but it wasn't for me. Still try to get in the pool every day, though. It's like, my therapy."

"Mmm-hmm," I said, knowing he wasn't actually looking for a response. He was looking for an audience. Fine by me. The less I talked, the less he'd know about me. Or the MacFarlanes.

"So!" he said, suddenly clapping his hands together

and nearly making me jump. "Your dad said you were bringing me something?"

I noticed how he didn't specifically mention the money. Or even more accurately, our bribe.

"Yeah," I said, motioning to my backpack with a jerk of my hand. "But can I use your bathroom first? I drank a whole Gatorade on the way over here and my bladder's screaming. I woulda peed in your moat, but well, now I know it's a pool, so . . ."

I shrugged like this was a suitable explanation.

He scrunched up his nose like he could smell something fowl, but then slapped a grin on his face.

"No problem," he said, even though I could tell he'd been hoping to take care of our transaction outside.

He led me through the tunnel and up to the tan-colored wood door. The handle was black iron, and there was a square piece in the middle with more metal holding it in place. I had to venture a guess that it was a peephole, even though the lighting in here was so bad due to the old-school lamplike lights on the walls, that there was no way you could make out anyone's features anyway.

"Where did your dad fly off to, again? Taiwan?" Mr. Admissions asked casually.

I cast my eyes to the side to catch a glimpse of his face. The guy wasn't as stupid as I'd originally thought. He was grilling me and trying to catch us in some kind of lie.

"Hong Kong," I corrected, repeating what Daddy MacFarlane had told him over the phone.

"Right," he said, just nodding. "What's he doing there again?"

I knew I hadn't given him any details of the fake trip so there was no way to catch me in a lie there. Best to just answer like your typical teenager.

"Don't know. Something for business," I said, letting my voice trail off as I walked into the foyer. This area was two stories tall, and my neck craned back as I followed the open space up to the very top of the house. Hanging from the ceiling was a chandelier that looked like plane propellers. And then I noticed there was something just above it.

"Whoa," I breathed. "Is that a—"

"It's the nose of a plane," he finished for me. "I had it installed after I crashed it on my fifty-seventh flight."

"Geez," I said, eyes wide as I turned to look at him. "For real?"

"For real," he said, face brimming with pride.

"You still fly?" I asked curiously.

"Every chance I get," he answered. "But now I fly one of those."

He motioned out the back side of the house to a landing pad that held a helicopter.

I tried to hide my surprise. People who were supposed to be as rich as my fake family was weren't amazed by things like this.

"Nice," I mentioned, before forcing my attention elsewhere so it appeared like I was unimpressed. I shrugged off my backpack and pulled out a fat envelope full of cash. He'd requested specific denominations, I assume to keep it out of banks, and in turn, keep the government from knowing how much he had coming in and from whom.

I gripped the cash and then tossed it underhand to him.

"You wanna count it?" I asked, standing back up and replacing my backpack.

"I'll do it later," he said, looking at me curiously. "I trust your dad."

"Dad says a good businessman always counts his money," I said, nodding at the wad of cash in his hand. "And that you should never trust anyone."

Mr. Admissions broke into a smile.

"Your dad's a smart man," he said. "Well, I suppose it wouldn't hurt to give it a count."

I shrugged like I didn't care.

"Do what you gotta do," I said. Then I gestured around like I was looking for something. "Where's the bathroom?"

Mr. Admissions pointed to a space just left of the entrance.

"Right in there," he said. Then he pointed to an area at the back of the house that looked out over an expansive back yard. "I'll be out in the courtyard . . . counting all this."

I nodded like I didn't care and turned to go into the bathroom he'd pointed at. When I dared to look back, Mr. Admissions was already out the door and heading toward a shaded area with comfortable-looking lounge chairs.

When I could no longer see him, I pulled out my security camera scrambler and pressed the button on it. Then I pushed it back into my shorts pocket and sprinted up the main set of stairs that wound its way up to the second floor.

Hitting the top of the landing, I continued forward, swinging a hard left into a long hallway and then taking the next hallway on the right after that. It was a maze that I'd memorized after looking up the blueprints of the house online. I'd tried beforehand to see if there were any rooms that would most likely be holding his valuables, or possibly even records of all his questionable dealings with other families.

I would need proof if I wanted to offer him up to the cops.

And I wanted to find his money so I could combine it with the Faux Four's loot fund for the new scholarship I was planning to open up for kids who couldn't afford to go to a state university let alone a private school.

There were two rooms on the blueprints that I thought might be where he kept all the things he wanted to remain hidden. One was downstairs, just off of what appeared to be his office. The other was upstairs inside the master suite.

I opted to check out the one that was currently as far away from Mr. Admissions as possible.

When I got to the master, I pushed open the double doors and then gasped as I saw the view. Three sides of the bedroom were floor to ceiling windows, the space jutting out like its own wing. I wanted to creep forward and look at the landscape below to take it all in, but I was suddenly aware of how visible I was, standing inside a see-through room.

So I kept to the back walls and followed them inward to the walk-in closet. On the draft, there was a room just beyond this one that hadn't been specified as anything. I assumed this was a secret room, not meant to be accessed by anyone but him.

And now that I was inside the closet, I was sure this was true. Because at first glance there was nothing in here except for clothes. Dozens of different warm-ups, some expensive suits, what looked like a whole line of golf attire, and tennis shoes in all colors and styles.

But no entrance to another room.

"Come out, come out, wherever you are," I whispered as I began to run my hands along the outer part of the closet, searching for switches or panels that might be false. When I got to the back where his shoes were perfectly displayed on shelves like a book fan might showcase their collection, I gripped the sides and swung them toward me like doors.

Which is what they actually were.

"Well, hello!" I said, breaking into a smile.

Just behind the doors masquerading as shoe shelves was another door, this one a beautiful black matte color with intricate detailing on its front. Unlike the shoe door, this one was ajar, open just enough for me to peek inside.

As I was leaning in to do just this, I caught a glimpse at the other side of the door, which was made completely of steel.

I froze.

This wasn't Mr. Admissions's safe or his secret treasure room at all.

This was his panic room.

Entry Twenty-Seven

There are really only two reasons a person might have a panic room. Either they are super paranoid and want to be totally prepared when the zombie apocalypse eventually happens. Or there's, quite simply, a *reason* for the person to panic.

Meaning: someone is after them.

Or if they aren't right now, they will be one day.

I'd met plenty of eccentric millionaires whose whole houses were tricked out to keep them safe from whatever they thought was out to get them—hostage takers, burglars, crazy people. The panic room was meant to keep them and their valuables safe in case that somebody came after them.

As I looked around the room, I realized that Mr. Admissions fully expected to be somebody's target someday.

He just had no idea that he was mine.

• • •

Uncle Scotty was waiting on the porch when I got home a few hours later. As I ambled up the walkway, I noticed that today, he was alone.

And I immediately felt a stab of guilt.

I slid my bag, which once again safely held my teenage boy costume, off my shoulder and dropped it to the ground next to the bench. Then I sat down with a loud sigh.

Uncle Scotty's eyes remained on the street in front of us. I turned mine to try to find what he was staring at, but there was nothing remarkable there. Still, I trusted that there was a reason his focus was out there, so I kept mine pointed in the same direction.

I needed to say something. To apologize for how I'd acted. For possibly screwing up what might've been the only relationship he'd had in forever. For being selfish.

But it was hard to find the words.

Just when I was about to at least try, Uncle Scotty spoke up instead.

"You know, there didn't used to be a stop sign there," he said, motioning to the red placard a few houses away from us.

My head swiveled to where he was focused. It seemed like an obvious place to have a traffic stop. What wasn't obvious was why he was telling me this.

"Oh," I said, not sure what else I was supposed to say.

"I tried for years to get one posted there," he continued. "I went to every town meeting. I put in requests to the city. I even spent afternoons out there with my own sign telling people to slow down."

I raised an eyebrow. I couldn't imagine a younger version of Uncle Scotty standing outside on his beautiful tree-filled block, holding a poster like a protester.

"Do you know how long it took to get it done?" he asked, looking over at me for the first time since I'd sat down.

I swallowed hard. I knew there was a lesson in this—with Uncle Scotty there always was—I just wasn't sure what it was yet. But I knew the story was about to go somewhere.

"No," I answered. "How long?"

"Six years," he said, finally letting out a deep sigh like he'd been holding it in most of his life. "And in the end, it wasn't even because of everything I did. Or tried to do."

"Well then, what did it?" I asked, knowing I was supposed to.

"A car finally hit a kid," he said, his voice flat.

I gasped.

"The girl ended up being fine," he said. "Broken leg, bruised ribs, some road rash. The stop sign was put up three days later."

"That's awful!" I said, imagining a kid getting hurt like that. Then I paused before saying, "At least you tried."

"I should've tried *harder*," he said, his voice frustrated now. "Every time I brought it up, the people said no. They said that they couldn't put a stop sign on every block and why should ours be any different than any other street in Greenwich. And then that little girl got hurt."

I placed my hand on my uncle's arm. "It wasn't your fault."

"I kept thinking that if *you* ever came to visit, it

wouldn't be safe for you to run around the neighborhood," he explained quietly. "I wanted to protect you even before you were mine to protect."

I felt the pressure building up in my face and knew that what would come next would be tears. But I didn't want to let them flow. If they did, I wasn't sure I'd be able to stop.

I hadn't known Uncle Scotty had thought about me at all during the years that Dad and I were traveling. That he cared about me any more than you did a relative you only saw every few years. But here he was, trying to get me a stop sign just in case I came to visit. He wanted me safe.

His niece.

And now, in a way, his kid.

"Everything I do is to protect you," he said to me quietly. "You've lost so much in your life, I didn't want to bring someone into our world who wasn't going to stick around. So, I didn't tell you about Kayla because I wanted to be sure. I didn't even care about me. I wanted to make sure that she wouldn't disappoint *you*."

"I—I didn't know—" I said, fighting to choose the right words.

But were there any?

"Uncle Scotty, I—"

"So, you guys *didn't* move!" a voice called out from the direction of the sidewalk in front of our house.

Uncle Scotty and I turned to see Ollie marching toward us.

When he saw our confused faces, he motioned to our

house. "Well, I figured the only sensical reason for why you suddenly ghosted me was that you'd moved."

I was both happy to see him and frustrated that he'd interrupted what I was pretty sure was going to be our family reconciliation.

"Ollie . . . ," I started to say, thinking that maybe I could join him upstairs in a few minutes after finishing up my talk with my uncle. But then Uncle Scotty cleared his throat and stood up.

"Haven't seen you in a while, Ollie," he said, stepping forward to clap him on the shoulder.

"Miss me?" Ollie asked, hopefully.

"The house was quiet without you," Uncle Scotty said, giving him a small smile.

"I'll take that as a yes!" Ollie exclaimed, pumping his arm in the air in victory.

A giggle burst out of my throat, surprising even me.

Uncle Scotty tried to hide his own smile, but had to turn his head to do it.

"Take it however you like, Ollie," he said as he began to walk into the house. "Just take it upstairs, would you? And quietly? I've gotten used to being able to hear my own thoughts again."

"Don't you get sick of hearing your own thoughts, though?" Ollie called out as Scotty disappeared from our view. "I would."

"Dinner in forty!" was all that Uncle Scotty yelled back through gritted teeth.

When we were alone, I looked at Ollie shyly.

"He was right, you know," I said, getting up from the bench, too. "It hasn't been the same without you around here."

"I can tell," he answered, following me inside and up the stairs to my room. "The vibe out on your porch was seriously depressing. You two still fighting?"

"I think we were actually trying to make up?" I offered, placing my bag on the bed and then unlocking the trunk where I kept all my thieving gear. When Ollie gave me an inquisitive look, I added, "The whole Kayla thing was a big miscommunication."

"Oh," he said, nodding knowingly.

I pulled my boys' black wig out and placed it carefully inside its case. Then I tossed the baseball hat and clothes into separate bags, labeled them, and then placed them carefully back in the trunk.

"You were working the job without me?" he asked when he saw the costume.

I shrugged. "Well, the con must go on," I said. "I couldn't just stop because we were . . ."

I didn't want to say what I was thinking for fear that it would start things up all over again. And we needed to stay on point if we were going to pull off the job we had in front of us.

"You couldn't stop because we were *fighting*?" Ollie finished, a twinge of jealousy in his voice. "Frankie, you were the one who ran out on me the other night. And it was only because I tried giving you my opinion and you didn't want to hear it. Like usual."

Ugh, so we were doing this. Again.

"What do you mean, 'like usual'?" I asked, putting a hand on my hip defensively.

"You know what I mean," Ollie accused. "Frankie, I get that you're used to doing your own thing. But you made me your *partner* and you need to start treating me like one. That means listening to me when I have something to say. And including me in the plan-making process. And letting me take point every once in a while."

"You *were* just in charge!" I said, exasperated.

Ollie gave me a look.

"That wasn't a job," he argued. "That was an *audition*."

"Okay," I conceded, though I didn't completely agree. "So, what do you want me to do, O? Turn this whole thing over to you? Let *you* go and rob Mr. Admissions while I sit back and watch?"

"Well, if it's good enough for me to do it, it should be good enough for you," he retorted. Then added, "*Partner*."

We both stood there on opposite sides of my bedroom staring at each other while breathing heavily from the stress of the confrontation. It felt like all we'd done lately was fight. And when partners fought, mistakes were made.

Dad and I had definitely had our own experiences with this, but when they'd come up, he'd just press pause on the job until we'd worked things out.

But we didn't have time to press pause. We needed to move forward.

"If you want to be lead on this, then fine," I said, knowing it was the wrong move, but not wanting to fight anymore. "Here's where we're at. We're not going after the Faux Four anymore—it would just end up hurting their kids more if their parents were sent away. Not to mention the humiliation they'd have to suffer when people found out what their parents had done."

"Even Brooks?" he asked.

I knew that what he was really asking was were we really letting Annabelle get away with no punishment too.

"Even Brooks," I said. When Ollie gave me a look of confusion, I added, "I read Annabelle's diary. Trust me, she's suffered enough."

"Okay," Ollie said, though he didn't look satisfied with my assessment.

His skepticism would have to wait. I had too much to catch him up on.

And so I did. I told him everything I'd learned about Mr. Admissions. About using Seth MacFarlane's voice as my fake dad. About posing as a boy to meet with Mr. Admissions. His house. His moat. His panic room. And finally, what was inside.

"Whoa," Ollie said when I was done filling him in. "So, we're taking down the big baddie."

I nodded.

"That's the plan," I said, lying back on my bed, suddenly exhausted.

Ollie let out a loud breath.

"Okay," he said. "I'm officially accepting the challenge."

He walked over to the blueprint of Mr. Admissions's house, which I'd taped up to the back of my closet door, and then hid behind the fluffy unicorn robe that Uncle Scotty had bought me for Christmas that year. The girliness of the gift was meant to be a joke between us since he knew I wasn't into pink or frills. But—and I'd never admit this to him—it had become one of my favorite possessions. And for now, it was a perfect hiding spot.

"When should we do this thing?" Ollie asked, looking back at me with excitement in his eyes. "Do we need costumes? I've been dying to try out a new persona I call Franco. He's this tough guy from the wrong side of the tracks, Brooklyn. You do *not* want to mess with him. He has a tattoo."

"Frankie and Franco?" I asked raising an eyebrow. "Really?"

Ollie rolled his eyes. "Well, you wouldn't be *Frankie*, of course. You'd be somebody else completely—"

"Still . . . *Franco*?" I asked disbelievingly.

"Don't poo on my parade," Ollie said, frowning.

"I'm not—*pooing* on anything," I said firmly. Then I added, "So gross."

"So, when should this go down? My schedule opens

up a little in a few weeks, so I could be available for a night of dispensing justice around . . . ," Ollie said, having taken out his phone and looking through his calendar for availability. "How's the nineteenth?"

"How's Saturday night?" I asked, bluntly.

Ollie let his hand and phone drop down to his side. "Please tell me you mean three Saturdays from now and not *this* Saturday night?"

"It's gotta be *this* Saturday," I responded, waiting for him to accept it and move on.

Ollie paced from one side of the room to the next. At one point, he stopped and turned to me like he was going to say something, but then closed his mouth again and continued to walk around. Finally, he stopped short and stared at me.

"Why does it need to be this Saturday?" he asked.

"Because it has to happen soon and . . . ," I said

"Aaaaannnnnd," Ollie prompted.

"And I already told Mr. Admissions that Daddy MacFarlane would meet him out that night, allowing us to break in."

I didn't bother to fake feeling bad about making the decision without him. It had needed to be done and Ollie hadn't been around to make his opinion known. I hadn't even been sure we were still a team on this.

Now we just needed to move forward.

"We good?" I asked him.

Ollie crossed his arms over his chest and shook his head. "I can't do it Saturday."

"Why?" I asked, frowning.

"I've got a prior engagement," Ollie said simply.

"Which is?" I asked, placing my hands on my hips.

"The cast is getting together for a bonding thing," he said, like it was the equivalent to having dinner with the president.

"So, skip it," I said.

Ollie's body stiffened.

"I can't," he said.

"You *can*," I reply. "Just bond with them some other time. You're an actor . . . *act* like you've bonded."

Ollie narrowed his eyes at me and took a step back.

"You're totally selfish sometimes, Frankie," he said, the words hitting me like a punch to the gut.

I let out a bark of laughter.

"Are you kidding me right now?" I asked him loudly. Then, I brought my voice down and said, "I'm doing all this *for other people*. By taking Mr. Admissions down, I'm helping those who can't afford better schools. And kids who deserve to get into schools but can't because the rich are always cheating the system. How is that selfish?"

"You're right," Ollie said, nodding. "*That* part isn't selfish. Your need to control things and do everything on your own timetable even when you know I have important stuff going on too . . . *that's* selfish."

"Well, sorry if I'm trying to look at the bigger picture here," I said, getting up and closing my closet door with a bang. "Maybe you should just sit this one out."

Ollie's jaw dropped open.

"You're kicking me off the team?" he screeched.

"Not *off* the team," I argue, though I briefly wondered if that was what I was doing. "More like, you can sit on the bench this time."

Ollie shook his head at me.

"I can't believe you're doing this to me," he said. "To *us*."

He looked so sad that I started to feel bad.

"Ollie—" I said, taking a step toward him. I wanted so badly to apologize, but he was already out the door.

Entry Twenty-Eight

I waited outside the gate until Mr. Admissions drove across his pseudo drawbridge and then finally left his estate.

I'd purposely set the meeting time between him and Daddy MacFarlane for seven thirty, since the sun set this time of the year by six forty-five, and I needed the cover of night to get onto his property.

As soon as the taillights faded away, I sprinted across the street, keeping my head down as I went. If anyone had been watching the road at that exact moment, all they would've seen was a flash of black. I'd special-ordered the outfit I was wearing for the job that night. It was a one-piece hooded jumpsuit that fit like a second skin and blended in with the darkness. There were thumbholes so you could literally hide something up your sleeve. A formfitting hood kept my hair out of sight, and more importantly, under cover so I couldn't leave any DNA behind that could lead to my capture. The suit was also fireproof, bulletproof, and because you never knew when you needed to go, it had a 350-degree waist zipper for easy bathroom access. There were also about a dozen zippered pockets, making it easy to carry any tools you might need along the way.

It was the ultimate in thief gear, and this was its debut. Ollie would've loved it. In fact, I'd bought him his own suit for his birthday next month. It wasn't nearly as flashy as he usually preferred, but I figured that since it was meant specifically to blend in, he might let the blandness slide.

Especially because the suit totally made you look like a ninja.

The thought of Ollie brought a knot to my stomach. I hadn't liked where things had been left between us. And while I'd texted him a few times after our fight, none of my messages had gone returned. So, either he was super busy with musical stuff, or he was ignoring me.

Or maybe it was a little bit of both.

By the time Saturday had rolled around, I'd come to accept that I was officially doing this job solo. Not that I couldn't pull it off on my own. My skills were better than most thieving teams, and it wasn't like I was dealing with an alarm system as sophisticated as, say, the Louvre.

And besides, I probably would've done most of the work on my own anyway. Ollie wasn't exactly up to my level of expertise yet and I kept telling myself that he might've even slowed me down.

But the truth was, I'd gotten used to having a partner in crime, and sneaking onto a property just didn't feel the same without him there to have my back.

I shook my head to try to clear my mind.

Dad had always said, "Don't ever thieve, until your thoughts retreat." It hadn't exactly rhymed but it was easy enough to remember. Basically, it meant that you had to focus or you were bound to mess up.

And I didn't want to mess up.

Not on this job.

I walked along the perimeter of the fifteen-foot stone wall until I reached the entrance point that I'd decided on earlier: next to an enormous sassafras tree.

Wasting no time, I began to climb the tree, digging into its trunk with the same steel spikes that I'd used to breach the perimeter of Annabelle's house. Ordinarily, it wouldn't have been too difficult—I'd certainly climbed my fair share of trees, including the one outside of my own bedroom—but this one had a wide trunk, and I was carrying about thirty additional pounds on my back due to all the tools I'd brought.

When I'd finally reached a branch that was a few feet above the top of the wall, I threw my leg over it and sat down. Pulling a pair of night-vision goggles down over my eyes, I twisted a knob on the side and watched as the view in front of me got closer and clearer.

Spending the extra cash on goggles that also had binoculars built in had been a wise choice.

I scanned the property. This time, in the front of the house alone, I counted a total of nine security cameras and two motion-activated floodlights.

Mr. Admissions wasn't playing around.

Then again, neither was I.

Pulling out my security camera scrambler, I pressed the button and watched as the light on the box turned blue, signaling to me that the cameras were officially offline.

I retrieved Miss Spikey from where I'd fastened her to my back, and then took her excess wire and wrapped it tightly around the branch above me. Pulling on it to make sure it was secure, I turned and took aim at the house.

With a tiny *pfft* sound, the metal claw sprung out from Miss Spikey and soared through the air before embedding itself into the side of Mr. Admissions's stone house. The fact that it was all rock actually made it that much easier to ensure a good grip, though I'm sure that wasn't why the material had been chosen.

Fastening a pulley to the wire, I grabbed hold of the two handlebars that were now suspended overhead, and looked out toward my final target. Then I examined the moat that lay in between me and the house with trepidation.

"Here we go," I said finally and kicked off into the night.

I'd been zip-lining in almost every country that Dad had taken us to. We'd gone on ones across the tops of huge rain forests, as well as tiny ones set up on obstacle courses.

But I'd never been on one at night.

Over a body of water.

While breaking into a property.

The pool was lit up so that the water appeared almost magical as it wrapped around the estate. I had a crazy urge to peel off and allow myself to drop down into the crystal clear surface below. But since it was about thirty degrees outside, and it wouldn't exactly be stealth of me to go plodding along the hardwood floors of Mr. Admissions's house soaking wet, I held tight and vowed to play out the fantasy another time.

As the house got closer and closer, I scanned the ground for the best place to drop. Then with a silent countdown, I let go, making sure to bend my knees as I made impact, and then roll out of the landing like I'd learned in parkour.

Popping back up onto my feet, I hurried over to the tunnel that led to the front door. But when I got there, I didn't go inside. Instead, I climbed up onto a massive planter off the side of it, and then pulled myself up on top of the structure. From there, it was just a few steps to the base of the slanted roof.

Within seconds, I was scaling the top of Mr. Admissions's house, only stopping briefly at the peak to enjoy the view before traveling back down the other side and to a rectangular area that jutted out from the rest of the mansion.

I knew from my visit the other day that I was now standing just above the master suite. I also knew that Mr. Admissions kept the top section of his all-window walls open, to let the fresh air in. Which meant that this was how I planned to get inside.

I searched the area for something I could tie my rope to, and finally found a round pipe about twelve feet away. Securing it with the best knot I had, I let out the rest of the length of the rope as I walked over to the edge. Then I glanced down.

I was three stories up in the air.

If I fell, I *might* not die.

I'd *definitely* break a few things.

But broken bones would be the least of my worries if I ended up getting caught.

Still I closed my eyes and took a deep breath, feeling the air enter my lungs. Then I let it out and took another. If Ollie were here, he would've said something inappropriate to break the tension and keep my mind off of all the things that could go wrong. He'd have done something like hum the theme song to *Mission Impossible*. Thinking about this made me smile and I realized that my heartbeat had begun to slow. I reopened my eyes with a renewed focus.

Get inside.

Do not fall.

Then I lowered myself over the edge.

To my relief, the top windows were still wide open, and I threaded my body through the tiny space, and then slowly slid down the rest of the glass.

The lights in the bedroom were off, but the closet

bulbs were blazing, almost as if Mr. Admissions had left them on for me.

I tiptoed across the floor, by now out of sheer habit, and then moved straight through to the panic room door, which was still cracked open.

Just as I was about to enter the room though, I heard a sound from somewhere inside the house. I froze in place, waiting to see if it would happen again. A few seconds later it did. It was a far-off thumping noise.

Thump. Thump. Thump.

What *was* that?

I knew that I should just continue on into the panic room. That I shouldn't go off and investigate the noise. But I *had* to find out what it had been. If I needed to abort the whole plan altogether, I'd rather do it at the beginning than midplan.

Then, everything would be over. For good.

I forced myself to take a step away from the reinforced, bulletproof doors and head back into the bedroom. Treading softly to the door that led to the rest of the house, I popped my head out and inspected both sides of the hallway.

There was nothing there. Just darkness.

And that sound again.

Thumping and now . . . scratching?

I looked back at Mr. Admissions's bedroom wistfully but knew I wouldn't be able to concentrate if I thought that something was lurking inside the rest of the house.

So I crossed my fingers and took a step out into the hall.

My eyes roamed over the art that was displayed on the walls as I walked slowly down the corridor. They weren't by any means priceless, but each piece would've drawn a nice little sum. Still, not the reason I was there.

I continued forward, forcing myself with every step. When I came to the top of the stairs, I leaned over the side of the railing to try to catch somebody walking around below.

But nobody was there.

The front door was closed. Everything was exactly as it had been when I'd been there a few days before. There weren't even any shadows moving around in the dark.

I laughed out loud at myself for letting my imagination get away from me, and then turned on my heel to head back to the panic room.

And stopped cold.

Because this time, a shadow *did* move.

Only, it wasn't a shadow at all.

It was an enormous black and brown dog.

And it was pissed.

I took a slow step backward, noticing that the German shephard's eyes, which were a fiery red color, tracked my every movement. I raised my arms in front of me to try to stave off an attack, but it only made him step closer. His large jaws opened wide, revealing sharp teeth dripping with drool that glinted in the moonlight spilling in from a window behind me.

And then he growled. Low and threatening. A warning that I wasn't supposed to be there.

"Nice, terrifying doggy," I whispered, suddenly wishing I had something to distract him with. A steak. A toy. Anything.

But of all the stuff I'd brought with me, something that would subdue a dog was not one of them.

So, I ran.

I didn't slow as I got to the stairs, opting instead to hop up onto the railing and slide all the way down to the landing below. Somebody must've polished it recently because I began to pick up some major speed as I descended, managing to gain a few precious seconds ahead of the angry dog.

Even so, I knew it wasn't going to be enough. I had to find a place to hide. Or at the very least, I needed to seek out higher ground where Mr. Admissions's devil dog couldn't reach me. I opted for the latter and scrambled up onto the round table in the middle of the front entryway, nearly knocking over the ornate floral centerpiece that had been placed on top.

I forced myself to ignore the snarls of the devil dog as he jumped at me, his razorlike teeth snapping at my heels, as I desperately searched for somewhere I could escape to. But there was nothing.

There was no escape.

"Fluffy!"

The devil dog was barking so loudly that I almost thought I'd imagined the shout. But then, as if a switch had been turned off, the animal quieted and sat back on its haunches, suddenly docile.

"Fluffy," a man's voice said, gently scolding the dog in a way that implied he wasn't actually angry at all. "Now, is that any way to treat a guest?"

I didn't want to turn around. I knew without doing so that Mr. Admissions had come home earlier than I'd planned. But besides knowing that I was an intruder, he didn't yet know what I looked like or who I was. From his angle, with my back still to him, he couldn't even tell whether I was a girl or a boy.

And if he didn't know my identity, he couldn't ID me to the cops.

But refusing to turn around also made me vulnerable. It meant I had no idea what he was doing behind my back. Whether he was getting ready to attack or had any weapons that he planned to use.

"Face me," Mr. Admissions demanded as I was still trying to weigh my options. Then, he added, "Face me or I'll let Fluffy make you her chew toy."

I locked eyes with the dog who was still sitting on the ground in front of me obediently. She licked her lips like she'd understood every word her evil master had said.

Being caught by the cops or eaten alive by a dog? Which would be more painful?

Finally, I decided to take my chances with Mr. Admissions. He seemed like the less dangerous of the two.

As I began to pivot around, I pushed my night-vision

goggles down over my eyes, so that most of my appearance was hidden. No way was he going to be able to tell who I was from just my lips.

"Clever," he said, when I was finally facing him. "But I'm going to need you to remove those. I'd like to see who I'm dealing with."

I shook my head slowly, refusing to speak because that would at least tell him that I was a girl.

He obviously didn't like my answer, because he slowly pulled his hand out of his warmup jacket, showing me that he did, in fact, have a weapon on him.

"Suit yourself," he said. And then, just in case I couldn't tell that he meant business, he pulled the trigger and a burst of electricity shot out of the black cartridge he held in his hand.

I felt the probes make contact with my suit before I flew backward off the table, landing roughly on my back. My body convulsed as the electrical currents surged from the two metal pieces that had embedded themselves to my thigh and side. Finally, I stopped shaking and my body grew still.

Mr. Admissions walked slowly over to me, the sound of his shoes clicking across the granite floor as he went.

"Go on, girl!" he commanded, motioning for Fluffy to head back to wherever she'd been hiding in the house before finding me.

Once she'd trotted off, Mr. Admissions crouched down until he was leaning right over me. He placed the taser down on the ground beside him and pulled the probes out of my suit in big, jerking motions. Then he stuck his fingernail into his mouth as if in thought.

"What are you doing here?" he asked to himself quietly as he studied my still-covered-up face. "Did Bruno send you?"

Then, he began to reach down until his hands were clasping the goggles disguising my identity. Just as he'd begun to pull them away, I felt him jerk backward, and then heard another round of snapping sounds.

Was he tasing me again?

"Not on my watch," another voice said into the darkness.

Entry Twenty-Nine

The way the line was delivered made the person sound a little like a cowboy. But a fake cowboy. Like it was actually a bad accent? Then I briefly wondered if I'd hit my head so hard on my fall that I'd scrambled more than just my system.

Before I could travel any further with this line of thought, somebody was lifting my head and lying it on something soft and squishy.

"Wake up, Frankie!" the cowboy hissed loudly, this time, much less macho-like. I felt the faint sprinkle of spittle on my face. I wanted to wipe it away, but I still wasn't entirely sure who my mystery savior was, so I continued to act like I was unconscious.

Then, the person dropped the bad cowboy accent and added, "You better not be dead or I will legit find a way to ghostbuster your butt and trap you in a box or a lamp or something and torture you forever by making you watch the original *High School Musical* until you know every word by heart. I swear to Gucci, I'll do it, Frankie."

And that was when I knew who'd come to my rescue.

"Ollie?" I asked, pushing the goggles off of my eyes and staring up into the face of my friend.

"Frankie!" he shouted, and then fell on top of me as he attempted to scoop me up into an awkward hug. "Omigosh, please tell me you're okay."

I reached my hand up to Ollie's cheek and touched it gently. "You just spit all over my face," I said slowly before giving his face a few light pats with my palm. "Also, you trap a *genie* in a lamp, not a ghost."

Ollie rolled his eyes at me. "And you always have to be right," he said, sitting back onto his heels and reaching out his hand to help me up. "I guess we'll see who's right when you're in the *afterlife*."

I groaned as I got to my feet and rubbed at the back of my head.

"Are you okay? I thought you were a goner after he tasered you," he said, looking me over.

"The currents didn't actually get through my jumpsuit," I explained. Then I pulled at the material of my outfit. "Tase retardant."

"Right," Ollie said. "Of course it is. So, you're okay?"

"I'm okay," I confirmed.

I jerked my head around, suddenly remembering that just a few minutes before, I'd been cornered by Mr. Admissions.

"Where is he?" I asked, finally stopping when I saw a figure crumpled in a heap on the floor not too far away from where we stood. "What happened?"

"Well," Ollie said slowly, opening up his palm and showing me a tube of lipstick. "Let's just say . . . June made *me* a few presents too. He'll be out for a while."

I smiled as sparks popped out of the container's top.

"Is there nothing that girl can't do?" I asked, shaking my head.

"Gotta be honest, I didn't even follow that, because I'm thinking we need to get outta here. Like, the Flash fast." He motioned for me to follow him and turned toward the door.

"I can't go yet," I said to his back.

He stopped where he was but didn't pivot back around. All he did was groan.

"I was really hoping you weren't going to say that!" he said, his head drooping forward in defeat.

"Sorry, O," I said, sincerely. "I have to get what I came here for. Otherwise, think of all the people I'd be letting down. But you can totally take off, though. I'll understand."

"Oh, no," he said, wagging his finger at me. "Who *knows* what kind of trouble you'll get into if I leave again. Just admit it: you *need* me, Frankie Lorde."

This actually made me happier than I had been in weeks.

"I won't admit *anything*," I replied, narrowing my eyes and crossing my arms over my chest defiantly. Then I grinned widely. "Except that I wouldn't have anyone else as my partner. My *true* partner."

"Fifty-fifty?" he asked.

"Fifty-one, forty-nine?" I teased.

He gave me a disapproving look.

"Fiiiiine," I said.

We began to walk off toward the stairs to make our way back up to Mr. Admissions's panic room when Ollie chimed in from behind me.

"Also, I want my own jumpsuit," he added, pointing to my outfit. "Like that one."

"Yours is already at my house, O," I said without missing a beat. "Already at my house."

"I'll need to bedazzle it first, of course . . . ," Ollie said as we left the room, already forgetting that he'd just incapacitated a bad guy.

Once we were back upstairs, I led Ollie through the bedroom and walk-in closet and then up to the panic room entrance.

"You ready for this?" I asked him, my hand on the doorframe.

He nodded. "Are you kidding? Let's get this party started!"

I pulled open the door and we walked inside.

"Whoa," Ollie breathed as he looked around the room in awe. "This is the most organized criminal's hide-out I've ever seen."

"I know, right?" I said, strolling along behind him. Then, acting like a department store worker, I elegantly waved one arm to the right. "And over on this side of the panic room, we have cassettes of every deal Mr.

Admissions has ever done. Each client's name is listed clearly and captures the admissions bribes on tape for prosperity. And likely, blackmail."

The small tapes were lined up on shelves specially made to fit them, similar to how somebody might display their record collection. Each tape was labeled and placed in order of date. And none were out of their designated spots. Mr. Admissions was either super OCD, or he'd watched that popular show on Netflix about organizing your space.

"There are hundreds of them," Ollie said in disbelief. "And cassettes? How old *is* this guy? Move into the digital age dude. For real."

"Here are his latest," I said, swiping up a handful of tapes on the table in the middle of the room and holding them up for Ollie to see. "The Faux Four and Daddy MacFarlane."

"This his little black book?" Ollie asked, holding up a dark ledger in his hands.

"Um, I don't think that's what it's called," I said, making a face.

"What?" Ollie asked, innocently. "It's small and black and it's a book. Well, a notebook I guess, but still."

I shook my head before waving my hand over to the left side of the space with equal flourish.

"And on this side, we have our personal bank portion of the room," I said, before picking up a bound pile of cash and fanning through it so it made that satisfying thwacking sound that playing cards made when you shuffled them. I closed one eye thoughtfully as I placed the stack of bills up to my ear and fanned through them again. "There's roughly . . . ten thousand here."

"No freaking way!" Ollie exclaimed, dropping the ledger and rushing over to the wall of cash and taking up a few bundles in each hand. "I've never held this much money in my hands before. This must be what Scrooge McDuck feels like."

I raised an eyebrow at Ollie. "You know he's not real," I said. "He's a cartoon."

"Still," Ollie said, removing the rubber band from one of the stacks and then smiling devilishly before throwing the money up in the air. As it floated down around him, Ollie sang, *"It's raining cash!"* to the tune of "It's Raining Men" by the Weather Girls.

I stifled a laugh, because we didn't have time for fun right now. We needed to get what we came for and get out.

Before we were caught again.

Maybe this time for good.

"Focus, O," I reminded him, pulling a nylon sack out of my backpack and tossing it to him across the room. "Make like a *real* thief and start filling the bag."

With a wicked smile, he placed the sack on the floor and began to toss the mounds inside. Halfway through, I realized how much we looked like bank robbers. All that was missing was the dollar sign on the side of the bag and we would've been a walking stereotype.

"What's this?" I asked out loud as I walked over to a tiny safe that sat in the middle of the table. I tried to pull it toward me to see what I was working with, but it wouldn't budge. And not just because it was all kinds of heavy. I quickly realized that the stainless-steel material that covered the box had been affixed to the table.

Curious.

"Do you see a key anywhere?" I asked, looking around for any sign of one.

Ollie gave a cursory search but turned back to the money when he came up empty.

"Nothing over here," he said.

I got down on my hands and knees and began to look for any secret compartments or hiding places closer to the ground. As I examined the area directly underneath the table, my eyes darted over to Ollie for a quick second.

"Hey, Ollie," I ventured, cautiously. "I know you had your whole bonding thing tonight with the others on Team Musical. So why did you come here instead?"

Ollie paused briefly as I said this and then chewed on the inside of his mouth.

"I kept thinking about your dad," he said, surprising me.

"Huh?" I asked confused. "Uh, is there something you wanna tell me, O?"

Ollie snorted and then got serious again.

"No, I mean, you know how I'm totally going to play him in the movie about his life one day?" he said, like this had already been decided on by the powers that be.

"Sure," I said, playing along. "Of course."

"Well, I just kept thinking about how I'll obvs have to talk to him one day—you know, in order to imitate his mannerisms and get into his mindset and all—and when I *do* finally meet him, I didn't want to have to try to explain why I ditched his daughter when she might've needed me most," he said as he snuck a look back at me while stuffing the bag with cash.

"So, it was purely out of a need to stay on his good side, then?" I asked, raising an eyebrow skeptically.

"Not *entirely*," he said. Then he turned full-on to look at me. "You *never* turn your back on your partner. Your dad taught you that, Frankie. And then you taught me. And despite the fact that you can get a little one-tracked sometimes, you would never let me down when it really counted."

I stared at him a moment and then slowly walked over to where he was crouching. Then I collapsed into him, hugging him tightly.

"Uh, wow. Okay," Ollie said. "You feeling okay? You're not really a PDA kinda girl."

I sniffed, forcing back tears that were threatening to form.

"Looks like you're rubbing off on me," I answered before standing back up and adjusting my outfit. "Well, enough of that. This stupid safe has an old key lock, and I can't find the key. Something one-of-a-kind. I'm thinking

Mr. Admissions has it on him. I'm going to go see if I can find it."

Ollie looked like I'd burned his favorite outfit.

"Are you *crazy*?" he asked. "We have no idea how long he's going to be knocked out for. What we *need* to do is forget that tiny little safe, take this money and run."

"If it's locked up, when the rest of this isn't, that means it's *super* valuable," I explained. "More valuable than the hundreds of thousands in cash that's laying around here. I need to know what it is. I'll be quick, O. Promise."

Ollie let out a loud groan. "This is not going to end well!" he exclaimed. "Later, when we're sitting around—either in some torture chamber or in jail—wondering where things went wrong, I'm going to point out this moment. *This* is where it went wrong. Right here."

"Noted," I said, and then turned away from him and started back down the stairs, hoping he wasn't right.

Entry Thirty

Mr. Admissions was still lying on the entrance room floor when I got downstairs. Because of what Ollie had said, I'd half expected him to be gone, having disappeared somewhere inside the house only to pop up when we didn't expect it, like some kind of Michael Myers movie.

But there he was. In the same spot as before.

Hopefully still breathing?

I peered around the rest of the room just in case Fluffy had decided to come back for his master. But she appeared to be gone too.

So I padded down the rest of the steps and crept quietly toward my mark, kneeling down to see if he was even still alive.

I let out a relieved breath as I confirmed that he was, indeed, still alive, and then began to carefully rummage around his pockets for the key to the tiny safe box. After I'd looked in every possible hiding place on his old-school tracksuit, I began to wonder if he'd stashed it somewhere else. In a desk drawer. Maybe taped to the back of one of the pieces of art that he kept in his hallway.

But then another idea came to me like a bolt of lightning.

I rolled Mr. Admissions onto his back, cringing as his head flopped around like a rag doll. Then I unzipped his jacket, gripped the top of his shirt in my fists, and tore the material in half, exposing an intricately carved key resting against his pasty white chest.

I resisted the urge to gag at the sight of his saggy, old-man skin, and focused instead on snatching the key I'd come down here for. The chain it hung from didn't have a clasp, and it was too strong for me to break off, so I leaned forward and lifted Mr. Admissions's head so I could slip it from around his neck.

Setting him back down onto the ground, I brought the piece of metal up to my face so I could see it better. It was unlike any key I'd ever seen, with a series of six prongs, each with significantly different shapes and sizes. I couldn't even begin to figure out how to break into a lock that had a key like this.

I was still so mesmerized by what I was holding that I didn't see the hand reaching for my wrist until it was too late.

"I believe that's mine," Mr. Admissions said, gripping my arm in his. For an old guy, he was strong, and while I tried to yank my body away, I didn't get far. So, I went for the only weapon I had at my disposal.

I took the key that I was still gripping tightly in my hand and slashed it down across his face. He let out an ear-shattering scream, and instantly let go of my wrist so he could bring his hands up to his now bloody face. I didn't bother sticking around to see the damage I'd done. I knew that he wouldn't be down long, and when he did get up, you could bet he'd be coming after me.

And he would be pissed.

I sprinted up the stairs taking them two at a time, my brain moving just as quickly.

"O!" I yelled as loudly as I could. "Get ready! He's coming!"

I pulled June's stun gloss out of one of my front pockets and got the sticky liquid ready. As I tore through the bedroom door, I half expected to feel Mr. Admissions's hands grip the back of my clothes and yank me back. But he didn't, and I continued to run straight through the walk-in closet, finally catching sight of the panic room door. Ollie was standing there, one hand on the frame and the other holding the hulking bag of money he'd gathered while I was gone.

I pushed him back inside the room, knocking him off-balance, causing him to fall on the ground hard. A move I barely registered because I was busy brushing the gloss across the fingerprint scanner outside the door, making sure it was extra goopy.

As I took a step back into the panic room, I looked up to see Mr. Admissions rounding the corner of the walk-in, red-faced from anger and blood. He raised his hand, something metal glinting off the glow of the overhead lights.

He'd learned that his stun gun wouldn't work on

me and had gone for something more heavy duty.

"I'm going to kill—" he bellowed just before I closed the door in his face.

"What just happened?" Ollie yelled as I stood there, my hand still on the handle of the door.

I knew it would take Mr. Admissions a while to get in, but I couldn't seem to get myself to let go.

"Uh, he woke up," I said, still staring at the back of the door. I couldn't hear Mr. Admissions anymore on account of the soundproofing that had been done in the room. This was both good and bad. Good because I didn't have to hear all the ways he planned to make us pay. And bad because I'd have no idea when he was getting close to breaking in.

Which meant we had to move. Fast.

I turned around to find Ollie still sitting on the ground where he'd fallen a minute before.

"Yeah, I got that much," he said sarcastically. "What I meant was, what happened . . . to *him*? His face was all messed up."

I moved straight over to the tiny safe and placed my hands on top of it like it was the Holy Grail.

"Yeah, well, he startled me, so I sort of scratched him," I said, and shrugged. "With this."

I let the key fall from my hand, still holding the chain it was on.

"You found it!" Ollie exclaimed, clapping his hands together before scrambling to get up. "Well, at least all that out there wasn't a complete bust."

"I guess we're about to see," I said as I slipped the key into the safe and turned it, hearing the distinct click of the mechanisms falling into place. Then I slowly lifted the lid and peeked inside.

"That's it?" Ollie asked, making a face as he peered over the top and saw what was sitting at the bottom of the box. "Well *that's* not anticlimactic at all, now is it?"

I snatched the contents up and shoved it inside the money bag along with the ledger and a few of the cassette tapes.

"Uh, Frankie?" Ollie asked as he watched me hurry around the room. "Can I ask you something?"

"Sure, O, ask away," I said, my breath coming out in gasps due to the fact that I hadn't stopped moving since my run from downstairs.

"Did we just lock ourselves *inside* a panic room?" he asked.

"Yup," I answered.

"And the one person who *can* get in, is an angry criminal who is currently standing right outside that door?" Ollie continued, pointing at the panic room entrance.

"Right," I confirmed.

"Okay, great," Ollie said nodding as he looked around in a daze. "Just checking."

"Look, it's going to take him a minute to clean the lip gloss off of the fingerprint scanner," I explained. "But then he's definitely coming in here after us. So, we've got until then to break out of this room and then get the heck out of here."

"Yeah, and we should do it before the cops show up, too," Ollie added.

"What?" I asked, stopping to look over at him. "The cops?"

He grinned, despite everything that was going on.

"You've taught me more than just how to pickpocket, Frankie," he said. "I called the cops while you were downstairs and told them there was a guy who's been taking bribes to get kids into colleges around the country. I also might've said he was holding a few kids hostage, since I figured it would light a fire under them to get here."

When I continued to stare at him, mouth wide open in shock, he held a hand up to stop me from asking what I was about to ask.

"Don't worry. I used a burner. And I did some digging ahead of time and found out that it takes exactly twenty-one minutes for the nearest station to get their guys out here," he said, holding up his phone for me to see the countdown of the timer he'd started. It had just passed sixteen minutes. "So, we've got time."

"No, we don't," I answered. Then I jerked my hand toward the panic room door. "Not before he gets in."

"Oh, right," Ollie said, his grin from before fading. "So, what's the plan then? How exactly are we supposed to get out without being seriously injured?"

"We're going over his head," I said, pointing up. "Literally."

Ollie followed my gaze as I looked up at the ceiling,

both of us making out the faint outline of a square above us.

"What is that?" Ollie muttered as he squinted his eyes.

"Our exit," I said, breaking out into my own smile.

I took off my backpack and placed it on the ground, pulling items out one by one and lining them up in a row in front of me.

"See, the other day when I discovered Mr. Admissions had a panic room, I started to ask myself why," I explained. "And all I could come up with was that he was either scared that one of the people he was blackmailing would come to take him out . . . or he was afraid the cops would figure out what he was doing and come to take him away. Either way, he doesn't want the police inside this room. So, then he'd have to have *some other* exit strategy in place in case they came here to arrest him. Unlike zombies and apocalypses, burned clients and cops weren't just going to go away."

Ollie was shaking his head in admiration. "It's like you're *A Beautiful Mind*, but for criminal activity."

I rolled my eyes but continued.

"When I was running across the roof earlier, I noticed the outline of a trapdoor, realized that it was right above the panic room, and put two and two together," I said. Then I cocked my head to the side with a twinkle in my eye. "You didn't really think that I'd lock us in a room with no way out, did you?"

"I—psht, no way!" Ollie said, avoiding my gaze. "I never doubted you for a second."

"We'll talk about *that* later," I said, eyeballing him. "For now, we've gotta get out of here."

I motioned for him to give me the bag of loot while he climbed up onto the table that was situated below the trapdoor. Once he was standing, he reached up with his long arms and gave the square door a push.

It moved just the tiniest bit before falling back into place.

"You're going to have to jump, Ollie," I instructed. "And fast. Time's running out."

Taking this as his cue to hurry, Ollie bent his knees and then jumped like his life depended on it. As his hands made impact, the square slammed open and the back side of it hit the roof.

Suddenly I could see stars up above us as the cold air began to trickle inside.

Wasting no time, I hopped up onto the table myself, much more gracefully than Ollie had, and joined him several feet off the ground.

"This is where all that time spent in gym class is going to pay off," I told Ollie as I gestured to the hole above our heads.

"But I'm failing gym," he whined.

"Well, you can't fail this," I insisted. "Look, I'll help push you up, but you're going to have to do most of the work. This is ninja stuff, here. Don't let me down."

"Fine," Ollie said, gritting his teeth. "But if I break my coccyx—"

"Omigosh, again with the coccyx!" I exclaimed, holding my hands out in front of me and motioning for him to step into them.

A few seconds later, I was pushing his legs up and through the hole above me.

"Hey! I did it!" Ollie said, peering back down at me through the square in the ceiling. "Look at me all ninja-like. Did you see me?"

"Yeah, Ollie," I said, feeling like I might've pulled a muscle helping him. "I saw you."

Then I handed the bag up to him.

"Okay, now it's your turn," Ollie said, reaching his hands back down through the hole. "I think that if you jump high enough to grab my hands, I can pull you—"

"Go, Ollie," I said, jumping down off the table.

"What?" he asked me, confused.

"You have to *go*," I repeated. "Take the money and all the proof and go."

"What are you talking about?" he asked, starting to sound mad.

"I need to keep Mr. Admissions here," I tried to explain. "If he gets into this room, he's just going to destroy all this evidence and then the cops won't have anything to get him on. I need to keep him from doing that, otherwise he'll get away with it."

"But, Frankie—" he began to argue.

"Go," I ordered. "I'll be fine. I have a plan. And I'll be right behind you. Promise."

"But partners don't leave partners," he said, looking pained now.

"They do when it keeps the other one safe," I answered. When I saw his face, I added. "I have to do this, O. And you need to get that stuff out of here. It's going to change so many lives . . . and that matters more than staying by my side. Go and be a hero."

Ollie looked like he was going to say no, but then he gulped hard and stood up. I could only faintly see his outline in the moonlight, but I could tell he didn't want to leave.

But then he did.

And I was alone again.

With no idea how much longer I had until Mr. Admissions got inside, I pulled on the boots that June had given me, strapped them on tight, and then unfolded the magnetic mat until it was spread out on the floor just inside the door.

Then I began to fly.

When the panic room door opened mere minutes later, Mr. Admissions didn't even notice the mat as he stepped onto it. He was too busy looking for us. When he didn't see us inside the room, his head immediately tilted upward and saw that the escape hatch was open.

He'd just begun to curse when I dropped down on top of him from where I'd been floating near the ceiling, at the entrance to the panic room. We both landed with loud thuds, my fall having been broken at least a little bit by the old man's body. He was so caught off guard, that he didn't even have time to register that he'd been trapped until after one side of the handcuffs were around his wrist and the other was around the stationary table leg.

"I know what you're going to say," I said, standing up slowly and brushing off my clothes. "Nice of me to drop in, right?"

I walked over to the magnetic mat and folded it back up before storing it away in my bag again. Then I hopped onto the table top and placed my hands on my hips like some sort of crazy superhero. I'd slipped my goggles back down over my face, so my identity was once again concealed.

"Who are you?" he asked through clenched teeth, the angry red mark bright across his face.

I looked at him and smiled. Then I jumped into the air, feeling the satisfaction when my hands gripped the sides of the escape hatch. Once I'd pulled myself through the hole, I poked my head back down to look at my mark one last time.

"I'm the girl who just schooled you," I said before dropping the door closed with a clang and running off into the night.

Entry Thirty-One

"This is torture," Ollie said, his face scrunched up like he was in physical pain.

We sat at a table in Grigg Street a few days later, waiting for the rest of our party to join us. Ollie had been complaining and fidgeting like he had ants in his pants since we'd sat down, and it was starting to make me feel squirmy too.

"If you think *this* is torture, then you probably shouldn't sign up for the military," I said, drumming my fingers on the table nervously.

"But it's *right there*!" Ollie said, pointing to the large pizza that was sitting in front of us. "And it's taunting me with all its gooey cheese and meat—"

"Stop looking at it, then!" I said, opting to turn my head away too.

"I can still smell it, even if I'm not looking at it," Ollie whined.

At that exact moment, one of the owners came over to our table and dropped a slice in front of each of us.

"I can't watch you suffer anymore," he said, winking at Ollie. "These are on the house."

"You are a saint, my good man," Ollie gushed before

picking up the steaming piece of pizza and shoving it into his mouth hungrily.

I rolled my eyes at him and turned to look at the owner. "Thank you," I said. "You just saved me from having to listen to a whole lot of complaining."

"No problem," the man said before turning back to the kitchen. "Figured you've earned a few slices, what with how often you guys eat here."

I held up my piece to him in a sort of cheers, before taking my own bite. As he walked away, I turned back to Ollie and changed the subject.

"So, we need to come up with a name for the scholarship," I reminded him quietly. "With the money we took from Mr. Admissions, we'll be able to put ten kids a year through school—private and college—for at least the next decade."

"How about the Ollie and Frankie Scholarship for Awesome Kids," Ollie suggested, his mouth full.

I paused at this and stared at my friend in disbelief.

"Or how about we choose a name that *doesn't* include our own, so that nobody finds out we're the ones fronting the money, and then starts asking where we got all the cash," I offered.

"Oh, right," was all he said.

I went back to thinking through names, and after a few minutes, I brightened.

"What about the Daddy MacFarlane Scholarship?" I proposed, smiling.

"Seems appropriate," Ollie said, nodding. "Especially if it gets back to Mr. Admissions that there's a fund set up with that name. It'll drive him bonkers."

"You mean more than he already is?" I asked, alluding to the fact that Mr. Admissions had been brought straight to a mental health facility after telling the cops who'd apprehended him that two ninjas had broken into his house and tased him before flying around the room and disappearing into the night.

"I can't believe he gets to wait for the trial in a place like *that*," Ollie said, referencing the cushy little facility that seemed more like a day spa than a locked-down looney bin.

"Doesn't matter to me as long as he's not roaming the streets or controlling enrollments somewhere," I said. "And with all the evidence they found in his panic room, no way he's getting away with anything."

Just like I'd hoped, Mr. Admissions—AKA Bill Sanders—had remained handcuffed to the table in his panic room until the police showed up. One look at the place and the cops called in the Feds before hauling him off to be booked.

According to Uncle Scotty, the FBI had already been looking into the so-called admissions coach after a few of his former clients had begun to sing—and *not* his praises. Turns out, we'd just sped up the inevitable.

"Ugh," Ollie said suddenly, making a face.

I turned to look toward the front of the restaurant to see what he was reacting to, and felt my face fall too.

"Are you sure we couldn't send her away too?" Ollie asked hopefully.

Annabelle swiveled her head toward the inside of Grigg Street at the same time I was looking at her, and we happened to lock eyes. She didn't seem surprised to see me sitting there with Ollie, but she also didn't seem happy about it. Still watching her, she snarled at me before brushing her blond hair over her shoulders and continuing on down the street.

"See? If anyone deserves to be sent away, it's her," Ollie argued.

I turned back around in my seat to face him. "Trust me, she's already being punished."

"You keep saying that, but I just can't see how it can be true," Ollie said. Then he gave me his sweet and innocent face. "You know, if you just let me read what she wrote then I could see for myself and stop bothering you about it."

I rolled my eyes.

"Yeah, right," I said. "If I gave you her diary it'd be plastered up around school in minutes."

"No way!" Ollie protested. "I'm *so* for a woman's right to privacy."

I gave him a look.

"For real! I mean, I totally know where you keep yours and I've never read even a page."

My mouth dropped open. When I recovered, I shrugged, trying to play nonchalant.

"First of all, mine's a journal, not a diary," I said to him. "Second . . . I guess I'll need to find a new hiding spot. Third, I just can't cross the diary line, Ollie."

I didn't add that I'd nearly done just that—until I'd found how utterly awful Annabelle's personal thoughts were.

"So, is *anyone* paying for their bad decisions anymore?" Ollie asked, crunching on his crust like he was angry at it. Then he paused. "I mean, besides Mr. Admissions."

"Well, kinda," I offered. "The other clients will probably be brought up on charges of mail fraud and the like. But, like the Faux Four, their kids probably don't deserve to pay for the sins of their parents. So, hopefully they'll be able to cut a deal if they turn on Mr. Admissions."

"So everyone gets a free pass," Ollie said with a slight grumble.

"Not a completely free pass," I corrected. "I took the Faux Four's tapes so they wouldn't be sent to prison and ruin their kids' lives in the process. But don't get it twisted. They're suffering."

Ollie snorted.

"Yeah, I'm sure they're just miserable over there in their multimillion dollar homes, wearing their Birkin bags and driving their Teslas," he said sarcastically.

I kept my head down, but raised my eyes to meet his. "You'd be surprised the kind of toll that guilt and stress can bring on people," I said slowly. "And trust me, they're feeling plenty of that. I sent Mr. Admissions's tapes to the Faux Four, along with a note warning them that if they ever tried to pull something like that again, the recordings would be sent to the authorities and they could deal with them."

"Oh!" Ollie said, surprised to hear about this.

"I might've also reminded them that they should focus a bit more on what's best for their kids than what's best for their public images. And if they choose not to heed my advice? Well, I kept a copy of the tapes for myself, of course," I said with a sly smile. "And believe me, they do *not* want people finding out the dirty little secrets that were on those tapes."

"Ooh, like what?" Ollie seemed to perk up at the thought of some juicy gossip.

I hesitated. Ollie was my best friend, and I trusted him with my life on the regular. But something felt wrong about divulging the skeletons I'd found in the Faux Four's closets. Well, technically, it was in Mr. Admissions' closet, but same difference.

It was true that most of what had been in their files wasn't all too surprising. However, one of them in particular had been.

That was the truth behind Sammy's family's empty bank accounts.

After meeting—and genuinely liking—Sammy's mom that day at her house, it had been super disappointing to discover that she'd gambled all their money away.

Eventually Sammy's mom had realized what she was doing and had stopped betting. But not before she'd racked up a lot of debt to a lot of people.

With this get out of jail free card I'd so generously offered her, I really hoped that Sammy and her mom could get back on track and keep their close relationship.

And that's why I couldn't tell Ollie what he wanted to know. Not if there was a chance Sammy's mom could make things right without her ever finding out and ruining their relationship forever.

So, I kept her secret. And the others.

For now.

"Trust me, you don't want to know," I said finally, making a face at him. "It will seriously haunt your dreams.'

"Geez," Ollie said, knowing it had to be bad if I wasn't telling him. Then, as I'd hoped, he moved on to another subject. "Is Mr. Derry back?"

"Yep. Got back yesterday. He was red-faced and well-rested," I said my smile matching his. "Funny thing though, our teacher didn't remember assigning us a project like the one the sub gave us. Imagine that."

I heard the door behind me open and after turning to see who it was, I sat up straighter in my seat, and forced a smile onto my face.

"And speaking of people who don't deserve to be punished . . . ," I said just as Uncle Scotty and Kayla sat down at the table across from us.

"Detective," Ollie said to my uncle, like he was addressing the president of the United States. "Kayla! Nice to see you both again."

I sighed.

"Hey, guys," I said. "Thanks for coming."

"Sure," Uncle Scotty said slowly, like he was nervous to find out the real reason I'd asked him here. "What's up?"

"I just wanted to say . . . I'm sorry," I said, forcing the words out even though it was embarrassing to admit them out loud. "To both of you for saying all those awful things and being rude. You guys didn't deserve it. I was just going through some stuff, I guess."

Then I turned my focus to Kayla.

"I think you might be the coolest adult I've ever met—outside of my dad and Uncle Scotty, I mean," I added, hoping that would win me some points with my uncle. "I liked you from the first time we started at The Farm. You treat us like we're not just dumb kids and I've always appreciated that. I guess I'm not used to trusting people outside my family—"

Ollie suddenly started to clear his throat loudly then. We all turned to stare at him, but he acted like he hadn't interrupted anything.

"Outside of my family *and Ollie*, of course," I added pointedly. "And I freaked when you accidentally called Uncle Scotty my dad. But that wasn't your fault. I have some stuff I still need to work through, and I'm going to."

Kayla smiled sincerely and reached out to squeeze my arm.

Then I turned to Uncle Scotty.

"And I understand that all you want is for me to be happy. And that's all I want for you, too. And if Kayla makes you happy—which you'd be stupid if she didn't—then I'm happy for you guys."

Uncle Scotty tried to fight back his smile, but I could see he wanted to.

"Are you sure?" he asked me.

I nodded.

"Totally," I insisted. "I think I just went a little teen-sane for a minute there. But now I'm back. With a peace offering?"

I pushed the still-steaming pizza over to them.

Both their eyes went wide and they looked at me like I'd given them bars of gold.

"You're forgiven!" they said in unison before digging in immediately.

"You guys want some?" Uncle Scotty asked, motioning to the untouched pizza that was still left.

I shook my head even while Ollie nodded his.

"We're good," I said, giving Ollie a look. He began to pout but followed my lead as I got to my feet. "We're actually gonna leave you two lovebirds alone and go meet June at Méli-Melo for some dessert crepes."

"Just be home before dark," Uncle Scotty reminded me before turning back to his pizza.

I was halfway across the room when I heard him call out my name. "And Frankie?" he said. "Thanks."

I smiled, and then pulled Ollie out the door.

If it was possible, it was even colder outside than it had been the past few weeks, and I pulled my puffy jacket up around my face until I could barely see where I was going. Linking arms with Ollie and walking side by side helped control the chill, but in the end, we ended up running until we burst into the French creperie down the street.

We were just looking around the place for June when I felt a tap on my shoulder.

"Hey, guys!" a familiar voice called out from behind us. "Sorry I'm late!"

We turned to see a grinning June, wearing an oversize pair of jeans and a sweatshirt with a picture of Einstein on it. It was so utterly her, I couldn't help but smile, too.

"Hey," I said. "We only just got here ourselves. Had to do some parental groveling."

"Oh," June said, looking interested but not prying for details.

That was the cool thing about her. She never pushed. Which, of course made you want to tell her things. I briefly wondered if this was actually a conscious tactic of hers—like reverse psychology—and vowed to think about whether I should adopt the same ploy in the future.

I forced myself to pay attention when I realized that June and Ollie were already deep in conversation and walking toward a table in the back. By the time I caught up to them, I had no idea what they were talking about, but I knew exactly what I was going to order.

Once we'd told the waitress what we wanted, we all pushed our heads toward the middle of the table and began to catch up. After a few minutes, I gave Ollie a look and he gave me a quick nod back.

"June, Ollie and I wanted to talk to you about something," I said carefully, a little nervous about what we were about to do.

"Uh-oh," June said, her face suddenly falling. "What did I do? Did you guys suddenly realize I'm not cool?"

I snorted. "Not at all," I said, shaking my head. "You're probably way cooler than both of us."

Ollie's head jerked in my direction.

"Speak for yourself," he said.

I rolled my eyes.

"Anyway," I said slowly before looking back at June. "We've been talking, and we think it's so cool of you to trust us with all your gadgets and stuff. And giving them up without even asking any questions about how we might use them . . . that kind of confidence in a friend is hard to find."

"Well, thanks," June said, looking sincerely shocked to hear this. "For some reason I just get this feeling that we're . . . a lot more alike than we realize. You know what I mean?"

"I think so," I said, though I highly doubted June was

the thieving type. "And that's why we've decided we have something to confess to you."

June's eyes grew wide and she held up her tiny hand to stop us.

"No!" she exclaimed, the word bursting out of her like she couldn't hold it in.

I flinched in astonishment. This had been the one reaction I hadn't expected from this conversation.

"I mean, I'm sorry, but don't say anything else," June pleaded. When she saw the confusion on our faces, she wrinkled her nose and stuttered as she tried to figure out how to say what she wanted to say. "I need to tell you why I was late before you tell me what you want to tell me. Then you can decide whether you *still* want to tell me what you want to tell me. Deal?"

Ollie and I nodded, our voices somehow gone.

"Okay," she said, taking a deep breath. "So, I'm late because I just got finished talking to some guys from the government—they didn't specify who they were exactly, but my theory is that they're from a certain three letter branch. Anyway, they just bought Who'sThat from me. For a bunch of money. You know when they took away the janitor at school the other day? Well, apparently it was because when that Alia judge put his photo through my app, all this crazy stuff came up about him being on the dark web. I don't know the details, but I'm guessing it was really bad. Anyway, these guys showed up today and told me that my app could be super dangerous if it was in the wrong hands and don't I want the good guys to have it?"

I had to admit, I'd had the same thoughts myself. There was a lot of power in being able to have every last bit of information on a person right there at the touch of a button. I would be in major trouble if somebody turned the camera on me, that's for sure.

But giving it to the Feds? I'm not sure that was any better.

"Anyways, I negotiated with them and now they own it. And I have enough money to put myself and all my siblings through any school we want," she said. "But that's not all. They might be sort of . . . recruiting me? For some special school for gifted and talented kids? And I have a feeling that if I decide against Alia and say yes, I would probably have to tell them about anyone who's breaking the law. Like, for instance if I knew a girl who was the daughter of an international thief and what she was up to. I feel like they might want me to tell them about that."

Ollie and I looked at each other, eyes wide open now.

"But I wouldn't want to do that," she said, trying to communicate something with her eyes. "And I wouldn't have to if I didn't know anything for sure. Does that make sense?"

"That's—" I began, before I was even sure how I wanted the sentence to end.

"That's amazing, June!" Ollie blurted out, reaching across the table and giving her a high five. "I mean, it could be an incredible opportunity. And good for you for getting paid!"

"Does this mean you'll be leaving?" I asked, surprised by how sad the thought made me. Sure, I hadn't known June long, but it felt like I had. I mean, for gosh sakes, I had just been about to tell her my secret, so I'd obviously thought this friendship was going somewhere.

June frowned. "I don't think so?" She answered it more like a question than a statement. "I don't know. We didn't exactly get that far."

"Oh," I said, frowning before I could stop myself.

"What do you think, Frankie?" she asked, trying to catch my eye again.

"Me?" I asked. "Uh, yeah, I think if you want to, then go for it."

"But I'm asking what *you* think," she repeated. "Like, would you do it?"

"No way," I said without hesitation. I saw the look on her face and backtracked. "But I might have a different relationship with the kinds of people you're talking about than most do. And I'm not so good with the trust stuff. You were sort of going to be my practice run."

I said this as I offered her a sheepish grin. The thing was, I did still trust her. Even with the new information about her possibly going to work with my enemies. In my gut I knew she was more like us than them. And that's what she was trying to show us.

That she wanted to find a way to make our friendship work while still following her dream.

And I was willing to meet her halfway.

"I think you should do it," I said, smiling. "I still want to tell you a secret, though."

"You do?" she asked, the excitement obvious in her voice.

"Yep," I said, leaning in conspiratorially. "You need to try the dark chocolate peanut butter crepe with crumbled bacon on top. It's not on the menu, but they'll do it if you ask."

There was a sparkle in June's eye as we sat back in our chairs. That's when I knew our friendship was going to move forward. I could tell.

If my relationship with my uncle was any indication, a thief could totally get along with a cop if both were willing to put each other first.

ACKNOWLEDGMENTS

All my thanks to those who helped make this book happen:

To **Bethany**, editor extraordinaire, for believing in Frankie and me enough to give us both a third book.

To **Reiko**, my agent, my gladiator, my champion, and also, my friend. You go to bat for me every time.

To my family: **Mom, Dad, Andrea, Price, Jacey, Amy, Cody, Oma, Ryan & Katy**, for your unwavering support and for letting me borrow little bits of each of you for my characters.

To my niece & nephews: **Cash, Riley, Robin & River**, for letting me be your cool aunt.

To **Natasha:** You're my beta reader, my throw-my-ideas-at-you best friend, and my Golden Girl. Thanks for reading this book before anyone else did and telling me you loved it (whether you liked it or not).

To **Jordana:** Our walk-and-talks allow me to decompress when I need it most. Your friendship makes me a better writer. Glad our boys are besties and glad we are, too.

To **Jordon**, my magical guru and soul sister, for your kind words and all the good vibes.

To **Kavita, Maggie, Jenny, Veronica & Sonia**, for showing my kids how to be kind little humans (and for putting up with them on the daily).

To **Huck & Grey**: You're the reason I write these books. You're both kind, mischievous, headstrong, clever, and brave boys, and I hope that you grow to be passionate and compassionate about the world around you. Always fight for the things you believe in.

To **Matt** . . . for literally everything. Thank you for giving me the space and encouragement to create these worlds.